Stories to Make You Blush

Marie Gray

Stories to Make You Blush

Seven Naughty Tales

Translated by Jane Davey

Green Frog Publishing

Canadian Cataloguing in Publication Data

Gray, Marie, 1963-
[Histoires à faire rougir. English]
Stories to make you blush : seven naughty tales
Translation of: Histoires à faire rougir.

ISBN 2-89455-081-2

I. Davey, Jane. II. Title. III. Title: Histoires à faire rougir. English.

PS8563.R414H5713 1999 C843'.54 C99-941807-7
PS9563.R414H5713 1999
PQ3919.2.G72H5713 1999

Translation: Jane Davey
Cover Illustration: Lucie Crovatto
Graphic Design: Christiane Séguin

Legal Deposit fourth quarter 1999
Bibliothèque nationale du Québec and The National Library of Canada
ISBN 2-89455-081-2

The Publisher gratefully acknowledges the assistance of the Province of Québec, through the SODEC (Société de développement des entreprises culturelles) and the support of the Government of Canada, through the Book Publishing Industry Development Program.

DISTRIBUTION IN CANADA
Prologue Inc. 1650, boul. Lionel-Bertrand, Boisbriand (Québec) Canada J7H 1N7. Tel.: (450) 434-0306

Green Frog Publishing is an imprint of Guy Saint-Jean Éditeur
674 Place-Publique, Suite 200B, Laval (Québec) Canada H7X 1G1.
Tel.: (450) 689-6402.

Printed and bound in Canada

City Lights

– That's it, the last box!

– It's about time!

Steve absently wiped away a trickle of sweat running down his temple.

– Do you really think we'll stay here for more than a year?

– We'll see... But right now, we've got to get a move on. We still have lots to do!

Another move; the third one in as many years. For some time now, Steve and I had been on an exasperating quest to find the perfect place to live. Our own home would have been ideal, but since Steve had been slated for eventual transfer to another city, we had agreed that this would remain a dream a little longer. So, full of enthusiastic optimism, I had spent three months systematically combing the city in the hopes of finding that "perfect gem", somewhere we could settle in for awhile until we were ready to commit to our little house in the country. And now, despite all the frustrating and fruitless searching, I finally had the sense that this was exactly what we had been dreaming of.

I had a good feeling about this apartment as soon as I saw it. After weeks of false hopes, false trails, and endless visits, I had been just about ready to pack it in. Then, one very ordinary morning, as I perused the newspapers without much hope, I came to an advertisement describing "A magnificent condominium, country calm near downtown. A real deal". Having read a ton of similar ads, I nearly passed this one over. But some strange instinct made me persevere anyway and before I knew it, I had unhooked the phone, dialed the number and made an appointment.

My excitement began to grow as soon as I arrived in front of the building. I was initially captivated by what I saw, then absolutely conquered once I entered the apartment. It was exactly what we had been looking for. First of all, the available apartment was at the very top level on the 20th floor, which eliminated the threat of unscrupulous people tramping overhead at all hours of the day and night. Next of all, the building was cross-shaped, featuring only one apartment per wing with the elevators situated right in the center of each floor. So, bonus feature: our next door neighbors wouldn't systematically be sharing their fights or favorite TV shows with us. What joy! And the list of advantages went on and on. There was a lovely park surrounding the building, which made for pleasant wandering outside in total safety. There was a guard permanently stationed at the entrance and – oh! what unbelievable luck! – the rent was very reasonable considering the size and location: only tiny budgetary sacrifices would be necessary. The building had just been acquired by new owners who wanted the place filled to capacity as soon as possible. They had sensibly lowered the rent and would probably keep it that way, at least until their objective was attained. We pounced at the opportunity – that is, I pounced at the opportunity... I was so certain that Steve would share my enthusiasm, that I didn't tell him I had closed the deal until he had seen the place himself. And he was just as thrilled as I was!

On moving day, our fatigue and the usual assortment of hassles didn't diminish our happiness. We liked the area, from what we'd seen of it so far, and we'd already met one of the neighbors on our floor. Her name was Diane and we both found her charming maybe a bit too charming judging by the appreciative glance Steve gave her ample breasts.

We had to slave for about four days before we could finally call ourselves "moved in". We had both taken some vacation time off for this purpose and I had to admit the results far exceeded our expectations, although the enormous size of the windows had caused us some problems. The living room and bedroom windows were so immense that our old curtains didn't even come close to covering them. Once we solved this problem, however, we were more than satisfied with the "look" of our new place and our supersized windows offered us a view so spectacular that we knew they had been well worth the extra effort.

We had our first candlelight dinner together on the fourth night in our new home. The meal and conversation were pleasant and the promise of sweet relaxation guided us out onto our magnificent terrace for a little fresh air. This particular July evening was warm and mild and a light breeze lovingly caressed our skin. There was still no trace of the heat wave that would be hitting us in a few weeks; it was simply a beautiful summer's eve, fragrant and soft.

We had turned off all the lights in the apartment so we could fully savor the incredible nighttime view from our terrace. Far below us, the city of flickering lights seemed surreal, and vibrantly alive. The traffic sounds were hushed and fluid, and the languorous strains of blues music began to travel our way from a neighboring apartment. We were finally relaxing and blissfully tasting the tranquillity of our new home. Our neighbor had left all of her doors and windows wide open to let the night air in, and although we couldn't catch any of the conversation, we heard a voice that was definitely masculine.

– Too bad for you, I teased Steve, she seems to have a boyfriend...

Steve smiled and moved his chair closer to mine. He put an affectionate arm around my shoulders, trailing his skillful fingers through my hair. A few minutes later, our neighbor's bedroom softly lit up. That's when we noticed that she had solved her curtain problem very easily: She hadn't put any up.

Although we hadn't meant to be inquisitive, we couldn't help but notice that her bedroom walls, previously invisible to us, were covered with mirrors. Since the window was almost as big as the wall that contained it, it would have been hard not to notice this particular feature.

– Not only does she have a boyfriend, they like to watch themselves...

Our neighbor slowly entered her bedroom door swiveling her hips in time to the music. Then she removed her blouse.

– There you go. Feast your eyes! My God, look at those tits! The bitch! What's going to happen when I'm not here? I'll know exactly where to find you if you aren't there to greet me at the door the minute I arrive!

I thought she was only going to slip into something more comfortable, or maybe change to go out; but instead, Diane left the room wearing only the skimpiest silk underwear. She returned soon after, pulling her boyfriend by the hand. After pushing him into the bedroom with a lively gesture, she made him sit down on top of what looked like a dresser. Lifting his arms up, she pinned his wrists against the mirror and began covering his neck and shoulders with sly, furtive little kisses.

– Hum, said Steve, this is getting interesting...

I sat there frozen on the spot... I couldn't say a thing.

Diane was now kissing her partner with increasing passion. She planted a volley of hot wet kisses all over the man's neck, shoulders, arms and torso while her slim little hands slid across his hairy upper body. He just sat there without moving a muscle. All of a sudden, she grabbed him by his wrists, swung him around, and then held up a warning finger to keep him at a distance. Through the window, we could see her from the waist up, but we could take in her entire body through the mirror. Diane climbed onto the now vacated dresser and began a sensuous dance to the rhythm of the music.

Her breasts were enough to make me sick with envy... and enough to cause my Steve to blush bright red right up to his ears. He just kept staring at her, a little shy but absolutely fascinated, not knowing if he preferred looking directly at her or at her reflection in the mirror. His breathing was getting noticeably more rapid and his gaze seemed to be glued to the scene before us.

– This is cheaper than a strip club..., he finally remarked in a voice that was tight with arousal.

At that moment, he pivoted his chair around so that he could easily slide his hand along my thigh, reaching my underwear faster than he might have wanted. Diane was still dancing, occasionally picking up and licking her voluminous breasts or teasing her friend by playing with her minuscule panties while a mocking smile played over her lips. Her thighs slightly parted, she pulled the sides of her panties high up her hips, exposing her glistening pussy as she furtively fingered herself. Her companion, obedient and submissive the way she wanted him to be, was rubbing the bulge in his jeans, having to content himself, for the moment, with just looking at her.

Steve had begun stroking me insistently in our corner. I was already very aroused. I was feeling a tiny bit – very tiny in fact – guilty about viewing the other couple this way, but I couldn't stop myself from looking: the display was irresistible. I sat there allowing Steve to fondle me, but I was barely aware of his presence as I selfishly savored the pleasure his hands were giving me. I could feel how swollen and wet I had become as Steve's fingers slid deep inside of me and quickly found their target. He rotated his fingertip on that tiny point of flesh inside of me. If he kept that up, the result would be the same as always: an impossibly swift and embarrassingly intense orgasm. Diane's lover got up and hastily removed his pants, revealing a cock with rock-hard purpose... and then he raised a finger to the light switch, plunging the room into total darkness.

We sighed in disappointed unison, but Steve still had the decency to continue until I came, which was almost immediately. I then noticed the enormous erection – which I hadn't deigned to take care of before – adorning his pants. It felt like pure iron! I couldn't leave the poor man in this condition, and I couldn't possibly waste such a gift. Licking my lips, I dropped to my knees before him and slid almost the entire offering into my mouth. I sincerely enjoy giving him this little pleasure; I do it out of love for him, of course, but it also gives me such pleasure... The power I feel when I have his cock in my mouth is indescribable: I become the true mistress of the situation, if indeed there is one. I began sucking him hungrily, running my tongue over his cock the way you do with a deep French kiss. Knowing that Steve goes wild for this stuff – what man doesn't! – I wanted to make the pleasure last as long as possible. So I sped up the rhythm of my wetly thrusting mouth by swallowing him as deeply as I could until I could feel his resistance giving way. He seemed surprised to feel me gradually slowing down, taking my time and then getting my kicks by feeling him go crazy as I tentatively licked and sucked him. I eventually let my hand gently take over. After a moment, I snatched him back into my mouth again and the tease continued. My lips were tightening over his quick-to-harden-dick, sometimes softly, sometimes firmly, but always insistently. Finally, on the fourth round, I allowed him to come and fill me with the fruits of my labor.

What can I say... there's nothing like a bit of fresh air! This apartment definitely promised many enjoyable evenings ahead.

* * *

I ran into Diane in the elevator a few days later. I felt the blush rising to my face almost immediately. I would be beet red in a second, but there was no escaping the situation. Feeling utterly foolish, I wondered if she would mistake my reaction for excessive shyness. She asked me if Steve and I were settled in now and if we liked what we'd seen of our surroundings so far. She confided that she'd always lived in upper story apartments and asked me how I found the view...

This last inquiry caused me to blush furiously... then relief took over when I realized that we'd finally reached our floor. She flashed me her warmest, most charming smile, and we parted ways.

* * *

It was the last day of our vacation... My, the holidays had gone way too quickly! I wasn't exactly looking forward to starting the same old work routine the next day. As we wanted to fully appreciate our last holiday evening together, Steve suggested that we begin by going to a little Vietnamese restaurant located nearby. Vietnamese cuisine was the first taste we discovered we had in common. We went out to eat it as often as we could, and we never seemed to get tired of it. As we had expected, the food at the restaurant we had chosen that night was wonderful, and we were happily impressed by the warm ambiance and quiet charm of the place. Our conversation drifted irresistibly back to the subject of our neighbor, and we began to wonder if, by chance, she had engineered the whole bedroom scenario knowing full well that we had been watching.

– Of course not, said Steve, how could she have known that we were out on the terrace?

– I don't know... But even from our bedroom window we'd be able to see everything.

– No way...

Steve hesitated for a moment.

– I've tried it already; it's too far away. The angle isn't right...

– Ah! I exclaimed, feigning outrage, I should have known you'd try to figure out a way to take full advantage of the situation!

– Oh, and I suppose you're going to tell me that you were horrified by what you saw, or that it left you cold?

– I wouldn't go that far.

We looked at each other and instantly, the common flood of pleasant memories gave us both the same idea: to get back home as quickly as possible!

I hate air conditioning as much as Steve does, so I immediately went to open the windows and the huge terrace door as soon as we arrived. The music emerging from the neighboring apartment leapt to my ears. It was hard rock this time. I left all the lights off and whispered to Steve to come over right away. Diane's apartment was aglow with a variety of colored lights. Two naked bodies, Diane and a different man from the previous time, were displayed in a setting that reminded me of a stage show bathed in red, yellow and blue. Diane was kneeling on the couch with her arms resting on the back. She was offering her back and buttocks to a gorgeous young stud with long dark hair and the body of a football player. He was, for the moment, standing still and looking at her, every muscle taut and alert.

– Let's go in the bedroom, whispered Steve, as if they could hear us. They're in the living room now, so this time we'll see them better...

– OK, I'm coming.

He was right; the view was just fine. Diane was keeping her position but the young man had gone into action now as he explored every facet of her body, masturbating himself with one hand while he fondled Diane's ass with the other. His fingers entered her with a gentle urgency as he ran his tongue over her arched back and willing behind. But one detail particularly fascinated me: the hand he was using to masturbate himself. It was a strikingly larger than average hand which only covered about half of his gigantic penis. I had never seen one that huge! Steve and I frantically whipped off our clothes and I immediately leaned against the window ledge, assuming the same position as Diane.

Steve began to mirror Diane's partner. He slid his eager fingers inside of me, probing deep and hard. I saw Diane's lover finally penetrate her; I couldn't help thinking to myself that a penis that size must be really painful... But what a sight! Inserting himself little by little, the young man took his time. Diane must have been waiting impatiently because she suddenly shoved herself against him, forcing him brusquely inside her. I did the same thing with my own lover and although he didn't have the same proportions as the other man, his powerful thrusting more than made up for the size difference. As we watched the other couple, we tried to synchronize our movements with theirs. I was totally captivated by the animal intensity of those two strong, agile bodies that were now gleaming with sweat. Diane's breasts were bouncing to the frenzied rhythm of their lovemaking and I could easily imagine, more than I could actually see, her lover's enormous shaft forcing its way deeper inside of her at every thrust.

The lover sped up his rhythm and Steve followed suit. Every staggering thrust of Steve's stomach against my body threatened to knock me off balance. I could see that Diane was having the same experience as me as she steadied herself against the force of her lover's ramming. Both men slowed down together, pausing as they clasped our necks and shoulders before grabbing us both by the hair to resume pumping harder than ever. We even appeared to come together. Steve then made me turn around and sit on the window ledge. He began licking my pussy with a vengeance, making me come one more fabulous time with his tongue. I didn't know what the other couple was doing anymore at that point, but I did have one tiny regret; in spite of the incredible intensity of what we had done, I still wished it could have lasted just a little longer...

– Do you think we should stop watching them? I asked Steve, who was still panting a little.

– Why? I don't see any harm in it... It certainly beats the movies we end up with...

– Absolutely, especially the movies you choose... Yech!

– I beg your pardon, Miss? You'll be making the selection next time.

– That probably won't be necessary anymore, especially if she changes partners every week... Although I must say... That one had a certain "je ne sais quoi..."

Diane did change partners pretty regularly. The boyfriend with the long dark hair returned to her place a few times afterwards but we always seemed to get back home just as the "show" was ending. Diane enjoyed herself – and how! – with this man for about two more weeks. Then one evening, I came home and caught them in the middle of a fight. He left shortly after that, slamming the door behind him and we never saw him again. How disappointing...

A few days later, I came home early from work and ran into Diane on the landing. She suddenly announced that she had a craving for Sangria and was going out to get some. Off she went and a short time later, she knocked on our door to invite me to join her. I accepted her invitation as Steve wouldn't be coming home until much later. I was also very curious about her, as I knew nothing about her except for a few interesting sexual habits.

We drank the Sangria on her terrace and chatted casually about different things. I learned that she had once been an actress but faced with an uncertain future in that profession, she had decided to abandon it. As far as romance was concerned, she confessed to me that she had been very unhappy in love at one point in her life and now she "wasted no more time". If after a week or two the guy didn't please her anymore, she would find another one who did. She also confided that she was actually afraid to stay with any one man for too long for fear that the sex would become boring. I could barely repress a smile at that last remark...

The afternoon went very pleasantly. Our conversation remained fairly superficial and I managed to keep my mouth shut about the bit of "espionage" Steve and I had perpetrated. After emptying a few glasses of Sangria, which left me in an enjoyably relaxed state, I took my leave on the pretext that Steve would be coming home soon.

The phone was ringing as I arrived at the apartment. Steve was calling to tell me that he was on his way home. I stretched out on the couch with a book and was about to start reading when the sultry sounds of jazz began filtering my way from Diane's place. I looked through the living room window and saw her on her terrace. A towel was wrapped around my neighbor's body and her hair was wet. She hadn't bothered to properly dry herself and the late afternoon light gave her skin a golden gleam. Her eyes stared straight ahead giving her an absent, almost melancholy expression. Laying down on one of her lawn chairs, she closed her eyes, and slowly pulled the towel off.

She had an incredible body... I had already seen her naked before, but now that she was alone, I could admire her without distractions. The feeling that she knew we had been watching her was unshakable. She turned her head towards me and smiled, having either caught sight of me or guessed I was there. Her hand slowly picked up the small watering can that she used for her geraniums and she coaxed a lazy little trickle out onto her skin. As her fingertips spread the droplets all over her voluptuous body, the breeze on her wet skin suddenly made her shiver. She closed her eyes and began tenderly stroking her now erect nipples. I could see the rise and fall of her chest as she breathed and the shivers that traveled up and down her arms, shoulders and belly were making me very aroused. Diane raised her arms and began massaging herself. She started with the back of her neck, then slowly moved around to her throat where those supple hands began a sensuous descent down to her chest where they stopped to tenderly rest over each breast. A gently nostalgic expression filled her eyes. As if they fully appreciated the contact with her hands, her nipples had stiffened even more, allowing Diane to kneed her breasts even more insistently with those long, apt fingers...

I had never been aroused or attracted by a woman before, and I don't know if I really was attracted to Diane, but her exquisite body and attitude of carefree sensuality stirred up a fire in me. I had no desire to caress her or make love to her but at this moment I was very conscious of my own body's need for a certain kind of touch. Staring at her now, I imagined myself in her skin, tasting the same sweet sensations she was giving herself as she ran her hands over her body. My eyes never left her as I undressed, and although I still had the unsettling feeling that she knew I was there, my body's state of arousal wouldn't allow me to consider my actions for even a second. I lay down, just like her, and placed my hands over my breasts, which were much more petite than hers but every bit as receptive...

She was getting bolder now, curling her fingers through the tendrils between those tanned thighs. Spreading her legs apart, she dug her nails into the soft flesh, leaving scratch marks similar to the ones I was leaving between my own thighs. With the long fingers of her left hand, she opened her moist lips while coyly licking the fingers of her right. Both hands then joined forces between her legs to conquer that intimate region. Her fingers were slowly studying the contours of her pussy which I knew must be soaking wet by now. She began to tease her clitoris and circle the opening of her glistening vulva, but she was stroking herself so slowly and my excitement had made me so impatient that I was having trouble imitating her rhythm. I always had so much difficulty containing the rushes of excitement demanding immediate release that my usual masturbation sessions always ended quickly. Through Diane's tutelage, I was finally learning how to give myself more than just a momentary orgasmic release. I was becoming conscious of my body's reactions to gentle and almost exasperatingly slow stimulation. Then, almost imperceptibly at first, she increased the speed of her movements. I watched her gentle fondling turn into frenzied stroking. Her face revealed every naked feeling; her sweetly distracted smile was soon replaced by a look of intense concentration before her face finally crumpled, fighting the unbearable pleasure of orgasm. Stopping suddenly, she forced her hands back up to her chest as she squeezed her thighs tightly together. Her face relaxed almost immediately. After a brief pause, she allowed herself to gradually re-enter the orgasmic flow, her arms crossed over her shoulders as if she was lovingly embracing an invisible partner.

Hesitating a little, she slid her hands back down over her belly and then further down still... She began dreamily stroking herself, her two hands united in a tender attack. I don't think she had even come yet. I felt so close to her at this moment, I was convinced that she couldn't, wouldn't come without me. As I began rubbing myself once more, I followed her rhythm so I could climax at the same moment she did... The water droplets sprinkled over her body reflected the warm glow of the descending sun... I watched her biting her lower lip... Low in my pelvis, the urgent stirrings of a huge, unstoppable orgasm were taking my breath away. I was just on the verge of letting it rip through me when Steve walked in.

He watched me for a moment in silence and then stepped forward only far enough to see what exactly had put me in such a state. There was an immediate bulge in his pants.

– Come here.

I interrupted my stroking before realizing that Diane had seen Steve arrive. She stopped her strokes as well and waited for the next phase. Steve knelt down at my feet and began kissing and caressing my legs, my thighs...

When his tongue slid inside of me, I could barely keep from crying out. My back arched, I was ready to explode. Diane was stroking herself faster and harder now. Her head was rolling from side to side as she struggled to contain the sensations. She got up and knelt on her chair, legs apart, back arched. Grabbing one of her breasts, she brought it up to her mouth while the other hand kept moving faster than ever between her legs. Knowing she was going to come any second now, I wanted to share the moment with her. I abandoned myself to the incredible sensations produced by Steve's rapidly flicking tongue and I begged him for release. He slid his hand up my leg and shoved his fingers deep inside of me while his mouth continued to flood me with pleasure. When Diane finally dropped her magnificent breast so that both hands were free to rock her into orgasm,

I came so violently my belly shuddered for what seemed like a full minute.

Diane was lying down again now; her entire body quivering. Steve couldn't contain himself any longer and in one violent thrust he was all the way inside of me. He impaled me with all his strength, shoving his cock deep inside of my body, encountering no resistance whatsoever as he pumped ferociously away. I got up and sat on top of him, guiding him inside of me so I could gain more control over the rhythm. I plunged him inside of me as deeply as possible and then sat very still, lovingly massaging him from the inside with skilful muscles... He allowed me to do this for about a minute before flipping me back onto the couch and draping my legs over his shoulders. He entered me brutally then, and didn't stop pumping until he finally exploded...

– So do you still think she suspects nothing?

– No...

– That really was a fine way to greet me...

– The pleasure was all mine!

Two weeks went by with no sign of Diane. As a matter of fact, we had seen nobody at her place since that last escapade. Steve and I were growing very disappointed, especially since that last "session" with Diane had been particularly mind-blowing. When we wanted to make love now, we always ended up peeping over at her apartment hoping to catch a glimpse of her, but to no avail.

As I was on my way to work one morning, I met the building superintendent who informed me that Diane would be leaving her apartment. He asked me if I knew of anyone who might be interested in taking her place. I told him I couldn't think of anyone at the moment, but that I would talk to Steve about it. I was saddened by the news that Diane would be going and I knew that Steve would be as well. No more nights of pleasure on the "observation deck"... Neighbors like Diane don't show up every day!

Well, we'd certainly lucked out for awhile, but now we had to face the hard facts: Diane was gone... although I must say, we sure had a few good laughs during the following weeks, watching all those people visiting the apartment. We tried to imagine what they could offer us in the way of the fine entertainment Diane had so generously provided. How about that couple in their sixties who barely looked at one another and appeared to be scandalized by the bedroom mirrors? Surely not! What about the burly man with a huge beard and tiny dog? Definitely not! The single woman and her three cats? I doubted it. The mother and her adolescent son who fought like crazy...? No way... The hand holding couple in their thirties with that unmistakable glow of newlyweds? Well, well...

It was in fact this couple who ended up renting the apartment. We never saw Diane again, not even on the day when an enormous moving van came to get all her belongings. A few days later, we invited our new neighbors over for coffee. They arrived looking tired, even a little haggard.

– Please excuse us, we've just finished moving in. What an ordeal... And those windows! Wow, you've really done a beautiful job with yours.

– Yeah, we had to rack our brains trying to figure out how to cover ours too. But the view up here is worth the trouble, believe me...

We chatted for a while and then they went back home. They were an adorably cute couple and were, as we suspected, newlyweds.

Steve was surveying the apartment with a thoughtful air

when his eyes suddenly came to a rest on my cute little dress. They instantly lit up with mischief. He looked just like a naughty little boy.

– Are you tired?

– It depends what you have in mind.

– I have an idea.

He went over to our curtains and pulled them wide open. Then he stuck on a blues CD and turned on our two favorite lamps. The room was filled with a soft amber glow. We heard the sound of our new neighbors stepping out onto their terrace to get some air...

Steve took me in his arms and began nibbling my neck and ears.

– What are you doing?

– Let's give our new neighbors a warm welcome, shall we?

And with that, he began pulling me closer to the window...

Feminine Impulse

I admit it: my history of disastrous relationship was probably my own fault. Ever since I was old enough to be interested in boys, I've always been driven to control events instead of just going with the flow. A new romance rarely had a decent chance to develop... If my love of the moment didn't correspond to my exact specifications, I'd get rid of him without further adieu. If on the other hand, he turned out to be exactly what I wanted, then I'd quickly classify him as much too boring and predictable and he'd be gone soon as well. After all, why prolong a dead end situation, right? I operated this way for most of my tantalizing teen, my terrific twenties, and a good part of my less than thrilling thirties as well. It was only quite recently that the sad and thoroughly depressing possibility dawned on me that there might not be, on this planet at any rate, an ideal man for me.

Although merely hypothetical at that stage, it was a disturbing notion nonetheless. Up until then, I had managed to convince myself, even as each new affair became more disappointing than the last, that I deserved the best of what the male population had to offer and that I would find my soul mate eventually, the man who would "fit me like a glove". My mother told me countless times that I would recognize Mr. Right immediately... So at each new encounter, I'd be looking for telltale signs (both physical and metaphysical), from stomach cramps to thunderclaps, from hot flashes to lightning flashes. When these omens failed to materialize, I just kept telling myself that the next one would surely be the right one.

But of course, it never happened. In fact, if anything, the men I met became increasingly wrong. This merry-go-round continued for a number of years as I moped, fretted, despaired, and witnessed, with infuriating helplessness, the appearance of my first wrinkles. I stubbornly insisted on believing in miracles and the power of positive thinking, but eventually I had to face the sad facts: what I was looking for hadn't yet been created by God, or whoever it was that had planted the human race on this Earth.

It couldn't be that unobtainable, I told myself. A list of the most important qualities a man had to have if he wanted to leap into my life had long ago been drawn up. It was fairly basic criteria. My self-image is very positive and well justified, so I have a perfect right to demand a certain number of attributes before I accord a man my favors.

This list of preconditions had been carefully recorded in a notebook so that I could refer to them whenever I forgot. This was to avoid the inevitable self-reproach: "I should have known!" that would come to taunt me after a few disappointing evenings with some candidate or other. To be fair, I did come across a few who measured up to some of my standards, but there was always something not quite right. Either he would forget that I hated broccoli and would make it for me three nights running (too bad, because the meal would have been lovingly prepared without me having to lift a finger), or he would infuriate me by giving me red roses after I had clearly indicated that I preferred white ones. I mean, were they doing it deliberately or what? Whatever...

After ruminating on the situation for many long nights in the company of my favorite vibrator, I finally came up with the solution to my problem. I knew at that moment that it was imperative that I stop looking for "The Perfect Man". It was essential for me to abandon the notion that I could find a single man, among mere mortals, who would fulfill my every desire and make me completely happy. So I ended up selecting... three.

Please understand that circumstances didn't leave me much choice. Besides, nobody was getting hurt... and I was doing myself immeasurable good. The ultimate irony was that I met them all on the same day – at different moments and in different situations, to be sure – but that night, as I lay down in bed, I knew at last that some truly interesting romantic possibilities awaited me. Only now do I realize how endless the possibilities really are...

For the time being at least, the three men in my life are wonderful. They manage to fulfill me, emotionally and sexually, in ways I never would have believed possible. They have absolutely nothing in common and that's precisely what makes them so appealing to me. They aren't aware of each other's existence, but they complement each other perfectly. And no one knows this but me.

One of them, Thomas, I compare to a waltz. He is tender and touching, romantic but solid. I met him at the supermarket and knew from one glance at his shopping basket that he was single. There was nothing particularly luxurious in that basket to be sure, but I could still tell he would be right at home in a kitchen, and I was right. Our encounter was quite comical in its own way. His arms were loaded with cheeses, milk cartons, eggs and butter. I kept wondering why he didn't return to his basket to unload some of those items. He was concentrating so hard on his shopping list that he didn't look where he was going and ended up tripping over my shopping basket. Eggs were broken, packages were spilled, and Thomas blushed crimson right up to his ears.

Our eyes met uneasily for a moment and then we burst out laughing at the same time. He suddenly confided, out of the blue, that he was nervous because his mother and her new husband were coming over to his place for the first time that night... Then to my surprise, he spontaneously invited me to come and have a cone with him at the new ice cream place nearby; after a few very pleasant hours of conversation, he asked me if I could save his life by coming over to help him through the upcoming ordeal with his mother and her new man. I accepted without hesitation and had a lovely evening.

Our relationship took about a week to define itself, the time it took to weigh out his good points and bad. I came to the conclusion that he could easily assume an important role in my scenario. He's an amazing cook and prepares me incredibly romantic dinners on a regular basis. Every three days, he brings me fabulous white roses or has them delivered to me. And I only had to tell him once what color I liked... Thomas loves going to the movies and he is one of those rare few, and so touching men, who can allow himself to shed a few tears during a sad movie scene. He displayed real tenderness and understanding regarding my romantic fate. After attentively listening to the story of my painful struggle during our first rendez-vous together, he tenderly massaged my back, shoulders and neck with his expert fingers. When we meet at my place, he always arrives a few hours before me. He washes the dishes, runs a hot bath overflowing with bubbles and welcomes me at the door with a perfect dry martini.

Before every first kiss at each encounter, he looks me right in the eyes and tells me in a voice charged with emotion, that I'm more beautiful every time he sees me. He adores my "voluptuous" body, or pretends to at least (let's face it, I could lose a little bit of weight) and treats it as if it was a gift from the gods.

Thomas is never in a hurry when he's in bed with me. His lovemaking is slow and affectionate as he covers every area of my body with his soft lipped kisses. He always makes sure the atmosphere is perfect: a few candles here and there, quiet music, satin sheets... Taking all the time I need, he builds me up to a delicious climax. Perhaps he's even a bit too tender sometimes... But this is not a serious complaint. I try to see him when I am most in need of his particular brand of tender affection. His penis is a little on the small side... but he uses it like a virtuoso. He slides it into me, almost shyly, after making sure that I've attained the right level of arousal. And he looks me straight in the eyes when we have sex, murmuring feverish words of love...

With Thomas, I feel like a woman, a beautiful and desirable woman. He knows how to handle passing irritability and unpredictable crying jags. He simply accepts them without question or comment. He was the first man who required no explanation for any emotional crisis. He knows exactly when to just leave me alone or when to console me.

This adaptability also allows Thomas to take my mood swings and continual indecisiveness in stride. This is a definite advantage since changeability is a female attribute I particularly rely on. He also knows how to listen to my confidences with a kind, benevolent attentiveness. I sleep like a baby in his arms, all fears forgotten. I always wake up in fine fresh form, feeling light and pleasantly carefree which makes for a perfect day ahead and plenty of leftover energy for... Rico.

Rico, a superb Jamaican mulatto, is a different experience altogether from Thomas. His skin is the color of a strong cup of coffee mixed with a cloud of smooth thick cream, and his powerful body is the product of a life spent outdoors doing hard manual labor. He's huge! He's at least two heads taller than I am, and all solid muscle. And, as an added bonus, he is more black than white between the legs... yes, in this case, the rumors are true.

Rico is a wild man with just enough class, gentleness and charm to make him the perfect escort. But I would never ask him to sustain a conversation of any depth, because in this department he can't keep his head above water for very long. When I have functions to attend, however, I strut around on his arm with no qualms at all! He's younger than I am but that's the least of my concerns... At every reception we've gone to together, the devastating effects of his brute sensuality are all too apparent. I've yet to meet anyone, male or female, who isn't affected by his charm. Rico's greatest appeal? His incredible appetite for lovemaking that time has done nothing to diminish. I would be very surprised if he ever lost this desire, unlike some of my previous lovers, although it's still a bit early to tell.

I know for a fact that some of the wives of my more "loaded" clients, women in their sixties who spend all their time working on charities and preening their poodles, would throw it all away – the home, the Mercedes, the jewels, EVERYTHING! – for a chance to spend even one night with Rico. And for all I know, maybe they do... Rico is a porno fantasy incarnated. He represents pure desire, heightened sensation, a brutal, fully awakened sensuality. But I'll get back to this point later...

And then there's Étienne: my daddy, my mentor and my idol. I'm his little princess, his gift from the heavens, his muse. Étienne is living proof that fifty is fabulous. He's never known anything but wealth and he is continually showering me with every imaginable luxury. He takes such obvious, almost perverse pleasure in doing this... Every night I spend with him is pure sophistication in stunning luxury. When he comes to pick me up, he brings me sumptuous gifts and outfits that look like they were designed for movie stars.

I met Étienne through my work. I had proposed an ad campaign – innovative, provocative and extremely expensive – to his associates. They of course advised him to wait for a less costly proposal, but he was instantly seduced by my approach and insisted on meeting me immediately. During our luncheon together, I knew without a doubt that he wanted to see me again, and not for the purposes of discussing his next ad campaign either... I loved my first night with him. We ate a fabulous meal in one of the city's finest restaurants, took a moonlight stroll along the river, had cognac at his place, and the rest is pretty much easy to guess...

He confessed to me that he was a fanatic for certain kinds of "innocent little pleasures". As far as he was concerned, women were queens who should rule over their subjects without mercy. Behind this feared business man, this unflinching boss, this well respected, ruthless giant, was a pliant, submissive creature who was ready to acquiesce to my every whim. One time he begged me to punish him for having imagined me in all sorts of suggestive poses, in all kinds of wild scenarios. From the very first night, I understood exactly what Étienne wanted from me. I came armed with my prettiest little lace apron and an assortment of stockings that I used to firmly secure his ankles and wrists to the four posts of his enormous waterbed. After that, I proceeded with some carefully calculated torture sequences, watching him grow harder and harder until his erection was bigger than either of us had thought possible.

He wanted to be punished and I couldn't in good conscience deprive him of this pleasure. Étienne is the kind of man who will not be denied something delicious. I therefore insisted that he make me come several times using only his tongue and a single finger... He did his best, the poor darling! I forbade him to touch me with his other hand, and I wouldn't even allow myself to graze by his body even if it meant having to use the utmost control in order to resist his caresses for as long as possible. I took pity on him after my fourth orgasm; besides, my knees were getting weak and my legs were starting to buckle because of the way I was kneeling over his head. I needed only to give him the slightest little lick with my moist tongue to make him come all over my face in a huge liberating spurt.

With Étienne, I feel strong, confident, and authoritative. Everything I do gives him pleasure: surprises, new experiences, the wildest fantasies... I can allow myself to live out any fantasy and indulge any whim I want. Once I got to know him after a few weeks, I knew I had to wait for the right moments to see him. Those nights when I feel strong and arrogant, or when I want to be spoiled belong to him. And I stay away when I feel like making someone else do all the work... Étienne adores me and thinks I am perfect in every way. He has a complete blind spot for the few faults I do have... And he's much too proud to impose any constraints whatsoever on me. I get no jealous rages from him because he knows who's mistress here and that my private life is none of his business.

In short, each of these men possesses different but equally incredible qualities. Seeing all three of them, allows me to enjoy fantastic romantic diversity, meaning I never get bored. I simply choose the appropriate one according to the kind of evening I want to spend. Never planning anything in advance, I wait until the last minute to decide which one I want to be with, knowing full well that whoever I choose will always be ready, willing, and just waiting for the least little sign from me. But with Rico, it's a little bit different...

I've spent about a dozen nights with Rico so far and each one left me with indelible memories as well as innumerable tender spots (temporary, yes, unpleasant, not at all...)

Rico is the only one I ever pine for, and the only one I allow to cause me any anxiety at the idea of making myself available to him. That's why I don't overdo it with him. I met him at the fitness center. The first time I laid eyes on him, I wondered if I was dreaming. It didn't seem possible that a man, and not a god, could exude so much sexuality without being either completely sleazy or completely gay. His body was covered in sweat and his dark skin glistened like some over polished metal. I stood there practically swooning for some moments before I regained my senses again... and then I quickly ran off to change into something a little more flattering. After making a few brief inquiries with some of the trainers – a number of whom had been Rico's ex-lovers and knew exactly where I was heading with my questions – I soon learned that he had been a model for several years. This had allowed him to support his passion for playing the saxophone without financial worry although he had no intention of making a career as a musician. He simply adored his saxophone and wanted the chance to play in eclectic little jazz groups from time to time. What did he do the rest of the time? He spent it looking after his body (and how!), skiing in the winter and mountain climbing in the summer...

Since I couldn't stop devouring him with my eyes, it took him no time at all to notice the effect he was having on me. And miracle of miracles, it was him I bumped into as I was leaving the gym. We chatted for a few minutes and then parted ways, but nothing had really started cooking at that point. This state of affairs remained unchanged for the following few weeks although Rico was always charming and solicitous to me. I figured he must have about a dozen girlfriends but I didn't let this idea discourage me.

It was a power failure that started the ball rolling one afternoon... I must admit that since I had met Rico, I was demonstrating a considerable penchant for exercise. Not that I had been lazy before, by any means... but suddenly I was putting in twice as much gym time as before. Strange wasn't it? That particular afternoon, I had even left the office earlier so I could arrange to be at the gym at the time I knew he would be there. The place was practically deserted when I arrived, but there he was, parading around in all his masculine glory. We began our exercise routine at the same time and performed our exercises at the same speed, although it's true that he did at times have to slow down his rhythm (just a touch) so I could keep up. Everything was going splendidly and once we finished our routines, we agreed to meet downstairs for refreshments after we changed. It was as I was heading to the showers that I suddenly found myself... in total darkness. The entire building had lost power.

I stayed glued to the spot, my leotard half down, wondering what would happen next. A few minutes later, I heard a trainer come into the changing room to tell the remaining few of us that it would be dangerous to continue any exercise routines and that we should make our way down to the entrance as soon as possible. Then he knocked on the shower room door and asked if anyone was there.

– I just have to get dressed and then I'll be right down, I told him.

It was then that I recognized the resonant voice telling me that a widespread blackout had occurred and the problem wouldn't be repaired for several hours. Rico... He was waiting at the door to escort me out. I decided I'd take a quick shower anyway before I joined him. I had just removed my leotard when I heard muffled footsteps coming towards me. My heart began racing but I managed to muster up enough bravado to ask:

– Who's there?

There was no answer, but suddenly I felt myself being lifted up by two strong arms firmly gripping my thighs as Rico gently murmured:

– It's only me. Do you want me to go?

My reply was to throw my arms around his massive shoulders and press my lips hard against his powerful, thickly muscled neck. His long tangled hair tickled my shoulders and breasts. I felt so small in his arms! He put me back on the ground and placed a finger to my lips to make sure I stayed quiet. As if I was going to protest! Then he took my hand and led me away from the locker room. I was naked but I couldn't have cared less.

The exercise room was empty and the only light source was the pale reddish glow of the emergency lamps. We were mere silhouettes in the mirror: a giant and a tiny girl. Picking up the girl, the giant lay her down on the exercise bench. He leaned over her and their bodies came together at a forty-five degree angle.

I was amazed by how soft his lips were, how fresh his breath was. But I soon lost track of that thought as I joyfully felt the delectable hardness pressed against my pelvis, a prelude to the pleasures to come. He was heavy, insistent, and his cock caused me delicious discomfort. I let his tongue explore my eager mouth, lick my neck and then my pert little breasts. Gripping the end of the bench, Rico ground his body against mine, roughly descending the length of my chest and belly before sliding back up to press his lips against mine once more. His skin was salty and smelled faintly of almonds and fresh fruit.

Picking me up once more, he carried me effortlessly, as if I was a little girl of negligible weight. What a delightful sensation! We came to another bench and he gently placed me on this. It was completely horizontal and equipped with supports. I felt myself being slid down until only my upper body was being supported. The rest of me, from the small of my back on down, was dangling off the bench. To keep from falling, I grabbed the bar over my head. I was almost afraid to guess what would happen next. I suddenly wanted to view the whole scene as a spectator, a voyeur. Turning my head to one side, I saw Rico's sublime body outlined in the mirror as he kneeled before me and spread my thighs. He paused for a moment to look at me, to look at the body that was laid out before him without a hint of resistance. I shivered at the touch of his enormous hands as he began to gently massage the soft flesh of my inner thighs, slowly inching towards his goal with two strong thumbs. I waited impatiently for those powerful thumbs to reach my pussy, which was now extremely moist. But he chose to avoid that spot for the time being. He massaged the surrounding area, opened and closed my lips, but refused to give me what I wanted. I felt the juices gathering like thick dew on my lips as he dipped a maddeningly gentle finger inside of me and brought it up to his lips. He tasted me with a groan of satisfaction. My own groans, unfortunately, were from dissatisfaction and impatience; once he realized this, his fingers came back to part my lips, exposing that tender area to the cool air and his gaze. He didn't move; he appeared to be thinking. Just as I was beginning to think nothing would ever happen, he shoved his tongue and an inquisitive finger inside of me. I sighed with relief. The mirror showed an image of a woman arching her back in the throes of terrible desire on a bench that was much too hard. I didn't want him to stop what he was doing for an instant... His finger was shoved so deeply inside of me it almost hurt, and his tireless tongue lapped up all my tears. I wanted to scream, but as we may not have been alone, the risk was too great. I had only one thought in mind: to grab him with both hands and shove him inside of me as far as he'd go. I desperately wanted to see if he was every bit as delicious as I thought he was. I wanted to be his prey... As if he had read my mind, Rico removed his shorts and rewarded my expectations with a gigantic, glistening cock that sprung straight up to attention. But my troubles weren't over yet... He stuck the end of his cock a bare half inch into my pussy and then pulled it out right away. He did this three times and then got up.

He found another bar which he placed right above my legs on the other side of the bench apparatus we were using. He slid my body far enough down to drape my knees over the bar, leaving my ass suspended in mid air over the end of the bench. He finally knelt down before me and in one movement, as if his cock was guiding him, he drove himself all the way inside of me, leaving me powerless before the onslaught. The mirror image I saw now seemed strange to me... There I was, stretched out on my back, arms up and hands gripping the bar over my head while my knees hung over the bar at the other end. I was completely vulnerable and at the perfect angle for my new lover to subject me to the full fury of his thrusting. And who would want to resist anyway? He was huge. It was probably the biggest cock I'd ever had in me. I was getting stretched wide open, filled to the limit, almost ripped apart. Even down on his knees the way he was, he was still heads taller than me. I could feel every thrust in my kidneys and numbness was beginning to set in my belly. Just as I was starting to feel that I couldn't take it anymore, he began sweetly caressing me to the rhythm of his hard driving cock, leaving me no recourse but to lose total control and come harder than I ever had before... But this wasn't enough for him. Later on, I would understand that what we had done up until then had only been "warm-up" time for Rico.

There was an apparatus for building up biceps in another corner of the room, in front of the wall-length mirror. It was a kind of seat with a cushioned arm rest that came to my waist, and it was just waiting for someone to come and make good use of it. Rico made me kneel on this seat with my ass perched nice and high in the air. The top of my abdomen rested on the cushion in such a way that my breasts were supported but entirely available for fondling. I was face to face with myself in the mirror. I could see my half-stunned look, my moist lips and my sweat-covered shoulders. Rico approached me from behind, his weapon pointing straight ahead. He guided himself inside me, penetrating me with all his force. My breasts lifted and shook with every blow as my stomach slammed against the cushion. Was that really me there, in the mirror? I didn't recognize myself anymore. I had become a spectator watching the most risqué of porno films where the heroine finally isn't faking it anymore.

The girl before me grabbed both her breasts and fondled them roughly while the giant behind her drove himself deeper and deeper inside of her, withdrawing every so often so he could then plunge himself back inside with even greater fury. This frenzied ritual continued until she could feel the urgent stirrings of another orgasm. As her muscles contracted, she felt shivers rushing all over her head and then there was a sudden flood of heat through her belly. She tried with awkward haste to reach between her legs knowing that the minute her finger made contact with the right spot, she would explode in a shuddering climax. Guessing her intentions, the man immediately slowed down... He wanted her to wait some more. Begging him to continue, she moaned in frustration. He picked her up from the bench and she wrapped her legs around his waist as he brutally re-entered her. It was he who performed the final act of mercy and placed a rough-skinned finger on her engorged clitoris. He felt the dam breaking inside of her as she melted into orgasm, and then he succumbed in turn...

Just then, we saw a flashlight beam and heard footsteps coming up the stairs. We made our escape into the locker room where we continued embracing under the shower.

Rico and I said our good-bys while I was getting dressed and our parting kiss was almost chaste. He left me pining for three days after that, but I couldn't afford to let him know how much I longed for him.

This first waiting ordeal seemed more like a week instead of a few days, but after that, we saw each other almost every day. Thomas and Étienne were getting worried, the poor darlings. I told them nothing and offered no explanations. After ten or so days, however, I started yearning for Thomas' tenderness again.

I phoned him up, quickly assuring him that I hadn't forgotten him and wanted very much to see him again. He was waiting for me with a lovely bouquet of white roses... A fabulous meal was simmering on the stove and the table was lit up with candles. There were no interrogations concerning my recent "disappearance" for the last number of days. He simply told me that he had been worried about me and was afraid something nasty might have happened. We spent the evening sipping wine in the living room and relaxing to the sounds of soft music. Then we fell asleep in each other's arms without even making love, which was just fine by me as my entire body was still feeling pretty sore... It was wonderful.

Later on, Étienne took me to the theater in New York. We flew in his company plane and the whole weekend had a honeymoon feel about it. We toured the museums and department stores where he spent a fortune on me. We stayed in one of the most expensive hotels in the city and explored all the possibilities of whirlpools, four poster beds, and stiletto heels. Étienne told me over and over again how much he had missed me. He said that he had been a good little boy during my absence but that he still needed to be punished for having masturbated a couple of times...

I inflicted him with one punishment after another thinking to myself all the while that I would really like Rico to give me the same treatment... We left each other at the airport, and as I sank down into the back seat of the limousine that was returning me to my place, I released a huge sigh of satisfaction...

I've been living this extremely full life for a while now... It's exhausting to be sure, but oh so satisfying! Sometimes I indulge in a few brief moments of solitude, although this is becoming increasingly rare. Since everything I desire is at my fingertips, being alone is an option I don't have to take. My life has become idyllic. Not a day goes by where I can't be seen with a satisfied smile on my face.

These kinds of experiences are all part of my work. I'm one of the lucky few who can combine business with pleasure and my work as an advertising designer is more fulfilling than ever...

The contract I was working on, the most important one I've had in ages, had to go off without a hitch. It was a highly coveted California deal and would be the crowning achievement of all my years of hard work. It would also guarantee my company's success, of course. That's why I conducted such an exhaustive research campaign and tested the product so extensively myself. The men in my life were absolutely amazing to me during this busy period...

Every good advertising designer has to know the product to be promoted inside out. So my motives aren't entirely selfish when I get so totally involved in the product testing end of things... I certainly benefit from it, and with a little luck I will continue to benefit for as long as I want...

I knew that I would soon be far too busy to see my three adorable lovers for awhile, so I decided to spend one last special evening with each of them. I would see them one at a time for one night only so that I would remain a little unsatisfied and anxious to see them again.

This time, I was the one who prepared a marvelous meal for Thomas. I didn't skimp on anything and offered him only the best. I worked hard from a menu I knew he adored and created a perfect atmosphere in accordance with his taste. Nestled in fresh satin sheets, we made love, slow and sweet. I drank deeply of his tenderness and affection.

The next day I dragged Étienne around on a leash for about an hour, and he delighted me by following my instructions to the letter. I strutted in front of him in my leather bikini and my dangerously high healed sandals. I felt gorgeously voluptuous, the *femme fatale par excellence.* His complete submission gave me immense satisfaction.

The following night, Rico and I made love with a vengeance in the dressing room of the tiny night club where he was playing. His music had thrilled me all night long and the desire I felt for him was almost more than my body could bear. He pounced on me at the end of the show and made love to me for what seemed like hours. I left him at daybreak, dizzy and weak-legged, walking dreamily back to my place so I could get a few hours sleep before I went to work.

It was time to say good-bye to all of them for now and get on with the work at hand. I had a huge, once in a lifetime challenge ahead of me but I felt ready to meet it head on thanks to the intensive one month product study I'd just completed. Sighing deeply, I finally gathered the courage to release the control lever and turn off the switch. I removed the headgear that connects me to the fantastic world of virtual reality, the most fabulous invention of the 20th century. I miss Rico already... the others too, and even the ones I've yet to meet!

Michael's Birthday

The Regency Hotel bar is one of those elegant, well-carpeted places with low key lighting and muted sounds. Plush velvet sofas and bar tables covered in crisp white linen are carefully arranged around the room. Airy jazz tunes float quietly in the background and the clientele is most often of the refined and sophisticated variety, especially at the beginning of the night. The place is usually packed. Business men, all kinds of professionals, and a certain artistic element as well crowd around the tables and up at the bar, and this particular Friday evening was no exception. There was an important fashion event scheduled to take place later in the hotel.

I arrived at the bar at 5:30 with my friend Christopher. He joined me on the pretext that he had to let the traffic die down before he continued driving home to the other side of the city. But I'm no fool. All he wanted was a glimpse of Gabrielle.

We parked ourselves at one of the few remaining available tables, ordered martinis and then sat back to unwind. The place was jammed... A typical hotel bar: every overdressed client was yakking away at their companions without paying the slightest bit of attention to the replies because they were far too preoccupied with getting noticed and holding their martini glasses correctly. After one sip of his drink, Christopher said to me:

– Are you sure this was where Gabrielle was supposed to meet you? I don't see anyone here wearing jeans...

– Get this. She promised me last night that she would "dress-up as a woman" for the event... She knows the effect that has on me... That's why she rented us a room.

The "event" I was referring to was really just my birthday, but Gabrielle attached a lot of importance to the occasion and she always threw her whole heart and imagination into making it a day to remember.

This year, Gabrielle began pestering me about two months before my birthday. She asked me for ideas to help her conjure up special pleasures for me.

– You, I said, covered in lace, with beautiful stockings and those high heeled pumps that drive me crazy.

– You're going to get that anyway! Go on now, think, what would really turn you on?

– Surprise me!

She said nothing about it after that. In fact, she made no mention of any plans at all... to the point where I began to wonder if she had forgotten the whole thing.

On the afternoon of the twenty fourth, one day before the fated occasion, she called me up at work to inform me that I would be spending the evening of my birthday with her. She also told me that she had reserved a room at the Regency Hotel where we would be dining that night. And if she still had the energy at the end of the night, she told me, she would force me to take off all my clothes, douse my entire body with champagne... and then lick it off me until she was completely drunk.

The whole concept sounded excellent to me, especially the champagne part.

She phoned me again on the day of my birthday while I was still at work.

– I have errands to run all day that just can't wait. What

time were you thinking of going to the hotel?

– Oh, I don't know... somewhere around 5:00-5:30.

– That's exactly what I figured... Let's meet in the hotel bar instead of the room, OK? I'm really sorry sweetie, but I don't know exactly when I'll be finished. Probably not before 6:30. I'm so sorry...

– It's no big deal. I'll just have a drink while I wait for you. It's my birthday after all... Who knows, there might even be a few damsels in distress to keep me company.

– OK, I get the message. I'll do my utmost to be there early. But if necessary, I will unceremoniously rip you from the arms of any forsaken women I find you with...

– Be gentle!

– Of course! I love you. See you soon!

So this is how I ended up here with Christopher who was sitting beside me practically drooling at the sight of all the women present. It was Christopher who had introduced me to Gabrielle, the woman I had left in charge of surprising me that night. He had tried to win her over before I entered the picture, but had failed miserably. However, he didn't hold this victory against me, even though he still carried a bit of a torch for her. That's why when I had mentioned the "dressing-up" she had in store for me, he was suddenly in much less of a hurry to get home.

– I'm not leaving here until I see what she's wearing!, he said.

– It's already 6:00 now... Where is she? It's getting late...

– She said she wouldn't be here before 6:30. Listen, it's hard for her, you know, trying to decide between her only two dresses...

My Gabrielle's wardrobe consisted mainly of jeans, camisoles and oversized sweaters. Sneakers were her footwear of choice except for the odd occasion when she wore cowboy boots. She rarely wore makeup and when she did it was very subtle. She almost never wore high heels except when she wanted to seduce me. Occasionally, and only for the purposes of pleasing me, she would wear some prettier, slightly more feminine outfits. She didn't have many of these, which was a shame, but what can you do...? She knew I couldn't resist those outfits when she did make use of them. At any rate, she had told me more than once that she simply didn't feel comfortable in what she called "female attire".

– I'm sure it will be worth a peek, I said. Gabrielle can look pretty damn good especially when...

But the sentence remained unfinished, and not just mine either... Every man in the place stopped talking instantly. No wonder! A woman who must have been some kind of movie star had just made an entrance, killing all conversation in one shot and staking her claim as the instant lust object of every man in the room. She was an erotic fantasy come true...

She had flaming red hair that fell in a fiery cascade right down to her waist. The long black dress that clung to her like a second skin was slit right up to the thigh, and she was perched on incredible black shoes with staggeringly high glass heels. Her nails were painted scarlet red, the same shade as her lipstick. And her only jewelry was a single strand of pearls, roped around her long, fragile, impossibly gorgeous neck. It was impossible not to look at her... not to desire her. She had the dazzling allure and imperturbable confidence of a top model. Her makeup highlighted to perfection her strangely exotic, almond green eyes and her fine eyebrows, which were the same red color as her hair. Even her glasses added a little touch of mystery. Her eyes were almost too green... and those lips!

Christopher was the first one to return to his senses. He shook his head as if to clear it and swallowed audibly while I stayed spellbound and continued to follow this mystery woman's every little move. She made her way to the bar where she sat down alone and made herself comfortable. I had the strange sensation that I'd seen her somewhere before. But where? I would never have forgotten meeting such a creature! After about thirty seconds of intense contemplation, I was already visualizing her without the dress, wearing only those murderous shoes, the silk stockings and her glasses. To my great dismay, I felt the urgent beginnings of a tremendous and undeterrable hard-on. Not even my rampant guilt would stop it, it seemed. I forced myself to think of my "sweetheart".

Attempting to override the presence of this bombshell, I summoned up images of the woman I have always found adorable even first thing in the morning when her face is all puffy with sleep. The one I never stopped loving for a moment, even when I came home from work to the sight of her slumped on the couch in front of the television, or when I found her dripping with sweat from an aerobics class, or acting like an irritating bundle of nerves at the steering wheel... I had never been unfaithful to her except on a few rare occasions, like this one, when I had been stunned by the presence of a young beauty and had innocently allowed my mind to wander a bit... What man could deny ever having indulged in such fantasies?

Christopher's thoughts must have been just about where mine were (minus the guilt probably) because he shifted his chair closer to the table and murmured:

– There should be a law against what she's doing... Phew! I know you're in love, but what would you do if a woman like that decided she wanted you, "you"?

I gulped in alarm.

– ... I don't know... but I'm hardly her type anyway, and besides that...

– Telephone call for Mr. Michael Peterson!

– Ah! Saved by the bell! It must be Gabrielle.

It wasn't Gabrielle. It was her friend, Dana, who informed me that Gabrielle was on her way and that I would have to be patient for a bit longer. She had just left Dana's place but with the kind of traffic there was right now, she probably wouldn't be here for about an hour. I was disappointed, but my disappointment evaporated as soon as I realized that the redhead was looking at me with what seemed like interest. No! I must have been imagining things... I went back to my seat trying in vain to control the blush that was already suffusing my face.

– Would you like another drink?

– Yes please, was it Gabrielle?

– No, it was Dana.

He was immediately sympathetic when I explained the situation and assured me that he would stay with me a little while longer at least.

– What are friends for!, he replied.

I wasn't sure how much friendship really had to do with it... but I thanked him anyway.

A waiter was approaching our table with a tray.

– Mister Peterson, the lovely lady sitting at the bar would like to offer you this drink.

– That's very kind of her, but I'm waiting for my companion...

– That's what the lady thought when she saw you on the telephone just now, but she'd like you to accept the drink anyway.

The waiter had a twinkle in his eye and I had a feeling he wasn't going to be dissuaded. So I accepted the drink in order not to offend the beautiful stranger.

I tried to catch the dream woman's eye so I could raise my glass to her in friendly greeting, but she was now actively engaged in a very animated conversation with another man whom she seemed to find charming. She didn't notice me. Christopher was suddenly irritable.

– Why is it always you? You, who has a fabulous girl already while all I have is my left hand and a pillow? Why?

It was now 6:30...

The redhead was still talking to the same guy, but he was starting to look quite tipsy at this point. It was completely obvious that he had only one idea in mind. Perhaps, I thought to myself, I should go and thank her for the drink now. It would be a good pretext to save her from a situation that was surely becoming annoying. I could ask the waiter to bring her a drink on me but with my luck, Gabrielle would arrive at exactly the wrong moment and I'd look like a perfect idiot. Christopher interrupted my reverie, saying that he had to leave. He made me promise to give him all the details if there was a sudden change in my plans tonight, and I knew he was referring to the redhead.

– Believe me, I'd like to... I'm going to give Gabrielle another thirty minutes or so...

I was getting a little fed up by this time. After so many tantalizing promises, Gabrielle had left me here to get bored silly on my birthday. I was beginning to think that she wanted me to sit here, in fact, and stew in the frustration of being lured by a slew of inadmissible enticements. Perhaps she had even set me up to test me against temptations that were practically inescapable.

All alone now, I could admire this stunner at my leisure. I kept waiting for her to turn her head my way so I could give her some small sign of gratitude. The man who was chatting her up finally gave up and left. She turned towards me but didn't look my way. She seemed lost in another world, in another bar, in another city somewhere. Then she suddenly cast a quick look around the room as if she was checking for the hidden camera or the perfect angle to strike a pose. She finally chose a position... From where I was, I could see the side slit of her dress widening even further, revealing the lacy stocking edges at the top of her thighs. One shoe was dangling lazily off the end of her toe and the movement was hypnotizing me. Without moving a muscle, I slid my gaze all the way up her body until it was level with her full breasts; they were resting against her arm and that arm was practically pushing them out of her neckline. I stared in fascination as one long strand of flaming red hair fell inside her velvet soft cleavage.

My own mind began to torture me by producing images of that strand of hair wrapped around my fingers. Should such hair be legal on a woman? My senses were acute but selective. I could no longer hear the din of the bar, just the roar of my blood as it surged into my crotch. I was blind to everything except that divine apparition... I imagined her floating above me in a huge satin-sheeted bed, her red mane of hair in my eyes, in my mouth... Oh! shit, I was hard as a rock.

Once again, I attempted to superimpose these fantasies with images of Gabrielle. My sweet, gentle, blond Gabrielle, whose short hair gave her an adorably tomboyish look. My extraordinary little Gabrielle, with her fantastic blue eyes, eyes so eloquent that talking was often unnecessary, especially in bed.

I turned away, blushing in a torment of confusion. She had read the desire on my face... So captivated had I been by her presence, I hadn't taken enough care to control my body language. That lipstick... on lips that were full like Gabrielle's, those glasses that gave her a look both serious and playful... It was enough to drive a man crazy. "Please show up Gabrielle, please show up so I can attack you like an animal! Please, come quickly!"

I risked another glance at this temptress. Getting up from her stool, she leaned over the bar onto her elbows as if she wanted to have a discreet word with the bartender. She whispered something to him before casting an innocent look in my direction. But it wasn't her eyes I was looking at... In the position she had now assumed, her breasts were lusciously pressed against the marble bar. She must have been completely conscious of my attention at that point because she began a little performance just for my benefit, or so I liked to think. She began swaying back and forth slowly and sensuously as she gently rubbed her breasts against the marble slab. It was like she was doing some kind of erotic dance... I watched her nipples becoming completely erect. She leaned her head against her shoulder and closed her eyes for a moment without interrupting her seductive little ritual. Her long fingers pulled an ice cube out of her drink and she placed it delicately onto her lips, like a kiss, before picking it up with her intoxicatingly pink little tongue. She let the ice cube melt on her tongue and run down her fingers, which she licked voluptuously while looking me right in the eye.

It was too much! I had to get out of there and fast; my own self-control and love for Gabrielle depended on it. I felt like I was part of some slow motion movie sequence where the background completely dissolves to reveal only the femme fatale in the process of seducing the powerless hero (me!) with her wanton wiles... She was almost going too far, but it seemed like I was the only one affected by her antics, maybe because her little show was in fact – amazing but maybe true – being directed at "yours truly". No one else in the bar seemed the slightest bit perturbed by what she was doing...

It was real torture, but I was helplessly caught in the trap. My body continued to betray me: I was harder than ever. There was no way I could just get up and move. Taking a deep breath, I turned my head towards the entrance in the hopes of finally catching sight of the one who had gotten me into this fine mess. But things were getting worse by the second... The redhead was coming my way. I shot another desperate glance towards the entrance. No Gabrielle in sight... And now the bar was starting to empty. She was coming closer now, striding gracefully towards me in spite of her impossible shoes, the slit in her dress parting at every step to display her long silky legs. And her nipples... so stiff and erect they seemed on the verge of cutting through her dress... and those slender red-nailed fingers that were wrapped around her glass...

She slid behind my chair and whispered in my ear:

– Your friend still hasn't arrived yet... May I join you?

A low, soft voice, with just a hint of a British accent. A sultry, spicy perfume... More quivering in my pants...

I kind of half got up and babbled:

– She'll be here soon. Any minute now, I'm sure of it...

– I wouldn't get up if I were you... Don't embarrass yourself on my account. Maybe another time, OK?...

– Oh, yeah. Sure, maybe...

She went around the table and stood in front of me in all her splendor before she slowly removed her glasses. Looking meaningfully at me, she bit her lower lip, just like Gabrielle... and then a mocking little smile began to play across her scarlet lips. Her proximity made me notice details that had evaded me before, and then, very slowly, reality kicked in. It can take a while for realization to dawn in a mind that's been paralyzed by desire. But I saw the truth at last. She was wearing tinted lenses and her eyebrows had been shaded with the same red color as her wig. I had never seen her wearing so much makeup, especially lipstick, but sure enough... It was Gabrielle!

– Do you want to keep on playing?

– Gabrielle! I don't believe it!

– You seem to like it... So, shall we continue?

– ... OK... but I can't get up!

– Why would you want to get up?

Putting her glasses back on she sat down in front of me. She placed her elbows down on the table, lowered her chest and began sensuously rubbing her breasts against the table cloth. I was fascinated, astounded, overwhelmed...

– How did you do it?

– Hey, are you playing or not?

– OK. Um, th-thank you for the drink you sent me back then.

– Think nothing of it. I was just passing through town and I don't see why a good looking man should have to wait forever on his own... I'd just like to get to know you a little while we wait for your companion to arrive.

I felt something slide up my leg. She sat comfortably back in her chair and ran her tongue over her lips like a contented little kitten. Then she smiled at me.

I was in shock. I couldn't believe it. She had completely and utterly transformed herself... But the physical and psychological effects that this unbelievable creature had produced in me were unchanged, except for the guilt which, to my immeasurable relief, had evaporated.

– You're not from around here, are you? I've never seen you before...

– No, I flew in from London this afternoon. Her leg slid even higher up mine.

– I'm here for the fashion show.

– Model?

– No, Photographer.

I couldn't say anything else. Both of her feet were now perched on top of my cock, which was as hard as it could possibly get, and those feet were gently kneading and massaging me, first gently, then urgently. I knew – and she knew it too that if she didn't stop soon, I was going to come uncontrollably in my pants, like some randy adolescent. Sweat was running down my spine and I was getting worried about what the other people at the bar could see. But her under-the-table antics were invisible thanks to the floor length white tablecloth. Gabrielle had no doubt factored this detail into her plan... She gave me some respite at last by pulling one foot away. Picking up her glass nonchalantly, she slid her free hand casually under the table. The glass came back down from her lips after a while and she looked at me for one long moment before lightly lifting herself forward. She brought her mouth close to my ear.

– Here, I have something for you.

She handed me the skimpy underwear that she had somehow removed under the table without my noticing, using that invisible technique known only to women. I took them from her and lifted them discreetly up to my face. Her perfume, mingled with the sweet musk of her body odor made me quiver.

Gabrielle held out her hand to me and I grabbed and kissed it, immediately smelling, then tasting her sweet, damp, heady perfume. I licked that hand fiercely. Pulling it away from me, she ran her own tongue slowly and sensuously between the fingers of that hand, sliding it afterwards along her throat, down her chest, then in between her breasts. Then, with a quick, deliberately careless gesture, she pushed my coaster onto the floor.

– You should pick that up, she murmured.

I leaned over and quickly checked under the tablecloth. She had hiked her dress up over her thighs, and through those long parted legs I could clearly see her glistening folds. She was running one hand under the edge of her stocking while the other hand was busily stroking her pussy. Those scarlet nails fascinated me... Her lips were swollen with pleasure and she was becoming hotter, wetter, and more excited by the second.

I couldn't hold myself back any longer.

– Come on, we're leaving.

– I haven't finished my drink yet.

– I can't take it any more

– I'm calling the shots here. Besides we haven't even eaten yet.

– We'll eat later...

– No. I've hired a special taxi to bring us to the restaurant. I decided we shouldn't eat at the hotel after all.

One look at my crestfallen face, however, made her expression soften and I could tell she would take pity on me and play it my way in the end.

She led me out of the bar to the hotel entrance. A long black limousine awaited us. Gabrielle ordered me inside and told the chauffeur to drive. The black partition between the front and back seats hummed to a close, completely isolating us from the driver's scrutiny.

– Where are we going?

– Oh you'll see. You wont be worried about where we're going for long.

She fixed her gaze on mine and slowly began pulling off her dress. But just the dress... She was now wearing only a black strapless push-up bra, the silk stockings, her shoes, and the pearls. Champagne being entirely appropriate, she reached for the bottle, popped the cork with one expert hand and poured out a single glass. She ordered me to drink it in a tone that left no room for discussion. She reached into her handbag and unfurled a silk scarf, which I was kind enough to let her tie around my wrists so she could then secure me to the door handle.

– Just to tease you a little bit, she reassured me. Happy Birthday, Michael!

She refilled my glass, took a mouthful of the champagne herself and then slowly released the liquid into my mouth. I felt it flow from her mouth into mine, slightly warmed and tasting sweetly of her. She licked a few stray drops from my chin and then began kissing me passionately – almost aggressively – as she flicked her tongue inside of my mouth, over my face and then down my neck. She poured some champagne onto her breasts and then licked it away, a sly little smile playing over her lips.

I could say nothing, do nothing... All I could do was watch her perform for me... and I had no intention of complaining! She poured a little more champagne over her breasts and then made me lick it off her so that I could taste the sublime, incomparable blend of champagne mixed with the sweet delectable taste of her skin. Every time she drank a little champagne, she shared some of it with me and the bubbly mingling with our saliva was a heady sensation.

Gabrielle sat down on the seat facing mine. She spread her legs apart and started slowly caressing herself again. Her scarlet-nailed fingers parted those tender pink lips so she could get down to serious work, and torture me a little more too, of course.

This woman of mine... who was also another... I would have given anything to be able to touch her, kiss her, make her come with my tongue and fingers. Her breathing was heavy with arousal as she stroked herself for a few more minutes and then suddenly stopped: she obviously felt herself in danger of reaching ecstasy too soon.

She finally knelt before me and began unbuttoning my shirt with unbearable slowness. Pulling off my pants, she started stroking me with only the lightest of touches, making me shiver with the violence of almost unendurable pleasure. I thought I'd be able to enter her at last... But then she told me:

– I want to look at you for a minute. I want to see you get impatient. I want to see you hard and ready.

Impatience was no problem!

But she didn't give me the much anticipated pleasure. Instead, she poured more champagne onto her body and began caressing herself all over again. The bubbly liquid ran down her breasts, over her belly and then down between her legs... She flicked off her string of pearls in one move. Holding one end in each hand, she ran them over her abdomen and then down between her legs where they soon got buried in the moist folds of her lips. She slid them back and forth inside of her, slowly at first, then more and more rapidly. I watched in wonder as the pearls began to glisten irresistibly from her pre-orgasmic juices. Wrapping them around her finger, she plunged them deep inside of herself with measured strokes that caused her to shudder uncontrollably. I wanted to be those pearls and slide myself into the deepest parts of her body.

I didn't know where to look anymore. I was almost gasping as my eyes shot up and down from the hands that lovingly fondled those tender, wet lips to the mass of red hair that seemed to caress her breasts, neck and stomach. I had never been this excited, even during my first sexual experience. As she watched me looking at her the way I was, she seemed completely gratified to know I was ready to explode at any second. Then finally, mercifully, she begged me to enter her. But I was still tied up, and for the moment, she had no intention of undoing my bonds! She stroked herself faster and faster, her pussy flowing with champagne and excitement. Her half-closed eyes and glistening mouth suddenly squeezed shut as her orgasm rushed upwards and violently consumed her. Her body jerked, her muscles contracted, and then her whole face contorted with pleasure...

She got up at last, undid the scarf around my wrists and then mounted me like a panther as the car raced down the highway at top speed. Her long red hair fell into my eyes and mouth, just like I had imagined earlier. I was making love to both Gabrielle and a European stranger! It was incredible, indescribable...

We made love wildly, frantically, the way we had at the beginning of our relationship, but it was even better now... I was having trouble holding back from coming. What a strange sensation! I was with a woman I knew better than anyone, knew every intimate detail about, but this woman was also a stranger! I stared at Gabrielle's blue eyes and saw them transform into emerald green cat's eyes. I was caressing my Gabrielle's body but this long red hair was completely unfamiliar to me. When she finally gave me permission to come, I yelled out "Gabrielle!", because it was indeed her I wanted and nobody else.

When we finally arrived home, I took her in my arms and kissed her with a passion that could just barely express what I felt.

– Happy birthday, my love...

– I love you Gabrielle. But I have a favor to ask of you... Do you think the British Miss could go now? I would really like to make love to the woman of my life. I feel guilty for having been unfaithful to her...

– I'll be back in a minute.

She went towards the bedroom, leaving me to admire the other woman one last time... and when she emerged a few minutes later, she was wearing her favorite dressing gown. It was my Gabrielle all right. My sweet, blond, adorable, generous Gabrielle. Seeing her once again – without makeup and looking suddenly so petite in her oversized bathrobe – made me desire her with such force that we didn't even get as far as the bedroom...

The Roar of the Crowd

For some time now, the reality I once knew has been dramatically altered. I now live in a world where limits have no place, a world where all my most outrageous fantasies can, and probably will, come to life. My days and nights are spent wondering what he will dream up next, and the wait is deliciously unendurable...

I should say a little bit about myself. I used to be what some people might have qualified as a "woman with limited prospects". After my last failed relationship, when Dennis dumped me, I spent two years alone. But make no mistake: in this case, alone really means alone. Oh, I did go out with a few men for a drink or two, but nothing much beyond that. My sex life, apart from the contribution of a few rather limited "devices", was completely non-existent... except of course in my imagination where the ever present fantasies were painfully alive and well. I never, however, intended things to be that way! Only, ever since the breakup, I couldn't seem to meet any man who made me want to start the game all over again, the game of course being that process of accepting the million and one compromises and weeding out the countless blind expectations that go along with the relationship package.

Friends and acquaintances alike certainly tried to set me up with some "good catches". But to no avail... After giving these set-ups a few tries, I decided to leave the chase behind, with no regrets. And then one fine day not so very long ago, against all my expectations, "he" waltzed into my life.

My good friend Renée, a talented painter, was holding her first important exhibition at a well-known gallery a little over a month ago. On a whim, I decided to buy three of her paintings, with the excuse that it would be better to buy them now while they were still in my price range. I immediately agreed that she exhibit them at the gallery for the duration of the show after which she would have them delivered to my place. The paintings I had chosen were truly wonderful depictions of couples making love and only later did it occur to me that having them around on a permanent basis might only stir up fires that were best left unstirred... Those intertwined lovers bathed in splashes of vivid, almost violent colour, their bodies an abstraction of lines and curves that conveyed both passion and tenderness were so...

Two days after the exhibition's closing, Renée inquired as to when I wished to have the paintings delivered. We agreed on a time that very evening, and she was right on schedule, in "his" company.

While opening the door, I had no inkling that my life was about to change dramatically. Renée was hiding behind one of her paintings and Daniel was standing there in front of her with a charmingly timid look that seduced me at first glance. The introductions were brief and I surprised myself by blushing like an idiot.

I took Renée aside into the kitchen to find out more about this unexpected apparition, leaving Daniel with the task of unwrapping the paintings. She was one of the only friends who had never tried to play matchmaker with me. She admitted that she had never thought about doing it until it recently dawned on her that her cousin, whom she saw fairly frequently, was in the same boat as me.

– You didn't tell him you were bringing him here for that reason, I hope!

– Of course not! He offered to help me bring back some paintings and when I told him I needed to deliver some to you, he insisted on helping me...

– Hum! Well, he certainly is cute... What's his story?

– Oh! he was married for four years and one day, his wife upped and left him for another man... but that was a while ago... He's completely over it now. But he's so shy!

– He's just adorable! So, what's wrong with him?

– Nothing that I know of...

And that's where we left it. We spent the evening skirting over a wide variety of subjects between sips of coffee. I was getting more and more certain that I wanted to ask Renée for her cousin's phone number. If he was really as shy as she said he was, I would probably never hear from him again if I didn't provoke anything. Suddenly experiencing renewed faith in my power to seduce, I still promised myself that I would wait a few days before making my move.

I didn't have to make any move at all. He phoned me the very next night to invite me out for a drink. I was quick to accept, and we've been together ever since...

Our first month together was the usual passionate beginnings: fascinating discussions, long walks, exhilarating visits, uncontrollable laughing fits, blush-inducing confessions... and flaming hot kisses. But only flaming hot kisses...

We had embarked on a strange adventure. We were in fact conducting a kind of "experiment" that had initially struck me as both pointless and sadistic, but after I gave it some thought, the whole idea suddenly became irresistible.

We had agreed upon one issue very quickly and that was our belief that a couple's first sexual experiences are often quite disappointing. And so, testing our newfound levels of "adult" wisdom, patience, and self-restraint, we pledged to wait a month before we made love. As it happened, during the short string of days of that month, we became so drawn to one another that we were soon entertaining the idea of a serious relationship – or at least a monogamous one – unless of course, we found the other's lovemaking techniques too disappointing to pursue. In short, we wanted to make sure that we were completely compatible on all other levels before we started our physical relationship. We also wanted the desire between us to reach such peaks of arousal that our first lovemaking experience would remain etched in our memories forever...

Well, these were the romantic reasons why we wanted to persist with this plan... but actually, our decision was also based on some purely practical elements as well: Daniel had found himself in some really awkward situations after jumping into bed with someone without taking the proper precautions; I had done the same thing a few times as well. Nothing a little trip to the doctor couldn't cure, fortunately...

But, all of this aside, we truly wanted our first night together to be perfect, and Daniel started his "research" right away. He slyly hinted to me that any clues I unwittingly gave him would quickly be picked-up and that one fine day he would serve me one of my secret fantasies in an unforgettable fashion. I'd tried many times to tell him that he really wouldn't have to dig very deep to find something to please me, but he was convinced that he could fathom desires I didn't know I had myself, and who was I to deter him on such an amusing mission... The results? Well, I obviously underestimated him, because ever since that time, he's never stopped surprising me sexually, and I'm always wondering what he has in store for me next...

All through the month, I wasn't allowed to be very explicit with my sexual clues. Otherwise his "offering" wouldn't have been much of a surprise. But I could tell from the sly confidence in his eyes that he was utterly sure of himself as far as my fantasies were concerned. On the day before the big event, he made me promise not to masturbate and not to try and see him that night.

All I was allowed to do was dream. The body I'd barely been allowed to touch would be mine inside of twenty-four hours. I hadn't seen him without his clothes yet and I endeavored to imagine him in all of his naked glory, trying as much as possible not to idealize him. He was a little on the thin side, and taller than I am by a good head. He looked like a student with his velvet jacket that was patched at the sleeves, and even more so when he put on his small, round reading glasses. Would he wear them in bed? No, surely not. Would he have muscular legs? Hairy ones? His arms and shoulders were pretty solid, as far as I could tell, without being overly muscular. He had a fairly slender waist, slim hips, and a small, round, firm behind.

As for his "thing", however, I wasn't allowed to go anywhere near it. But judging from what I had felt against my stomach when I held him close, it certainly was responsive...

I was very anxious about it all, but also terribly excited. What if he didn't live up to my expectations? I had initially told Daniel that my fantasies were a little "spicier" than the average woman's – at least that's what I liked to think – but

I hadn't elaborated that statement much. My view on "spicy" was that I ideally prefer settings other than the bedroom, and... I have a slight streak of exhibitionism that I'd never had the opportunity, or the audacity, to indulge. I'd always been attracted to the idea of arousing the greatest number of people possible. However, I would have to be certain that they would not be able to recognize me; orgies don't appeal to me at all, among other reasons, because I have no desire to damage my reputation. I often dreamt about unleashing my sensuality in public, but certainly not in front of people I knew or could meet in the streets!

It was a facet of my character, however, that I figured I'd probably never be able to indulge and the "good little girl" in me was certainly glad about that. In my mind, many women must dream about being desired by the largest audience of men possible, wanting to make their male spectators good and hard and reduced to the status of panting slaves. On the other hand, I am not sure that these women would appreciate the related "whore" treatment that might come with such a fantasy...

I had finally ended up dropping some more precise hints to Daniel about this secret urge of mine. He argued to unfairness, saying that his shyness – charming but sometimes paralyzing – would prevent him from ever carrying out such a fantasy. Feeling desirable was one thing, but in front of a crowd... No way! From what I could gather, his own fantasies were rather common: he fantasized about being accosted by two amazon goddesses, preferably twins, who would drag him into a wild menage a trois. I replied that it might not be impossible to realize this scenario but added that it was doubtful I could be involved as I had no twin sister... He also dreamt of watching two women making love. He had in fact asked me if I had ever been attracted to a woman before... When I told him no, he pulled a face and feigned disappointment. It had been his idea to serve me up something special. I, on the other hand, had promised him nothing out of the ordinary...

However, the way I was feeling at that time, I would have been very happy to see him arrive at my place any hour of the day so I could rip off all his clothes and make love to him in the most ordinary ways... in my bed, on my couch, or on the ground... I didn't care. I was so hot and bothered, I could barely sit still!

It was close to midnight on the night before the big day when the telephone's insistent ring interrupted my thoughts. It was Daniel...

– How are you?

– Impatient...

– Do you trust me?

– Yes, but I'm a little nervous...

– Nervous? Why?

– Maybe we should have waited until we knew each other a little better... What if it doesn't work? What if we're both disappointed? You know Daniel, I don't need to live out one of my fantasies in order to desire you. What I feel for you is deeper. I appreciate what you want to do for me but... what if it turns out to be a mistake?

– Hey, don't worry... You know something?... I'm already sure that I want to be with you no matter how our first night together turns out. We have so much to discover together... But tell me something, Miss Adventurous, are you chickening out all of a sudden?

– Not at all. I'm just feeling this weird mixture of curiosity and nervousness, that's all. I have no idea what you're up to... But Daniel, I want you here with me now, in my bed! I can't stand the wait anymore! I want to be in your arms right now... I want to feel your body against mine. I want to kiss you all over...

– Stop it, I'm getting hard... What are you doing now?

– I'm in the living room. I was watching TV so I wouldn't think about you so much.

– Take your clothes off.

– What? Why? Are you joking?

– No. Take your clothes off. Are you wearing a blouse?

– Yes...

– Go on then... Start with the first button and then slowly undo the rest. Imagine it's me undressing you...

Where had his paralyzing shyness disappeared to? Evidently, the distance created by the telephone was giving his confidence a much needed boost! I slowly undid the buttons to my blouse. I imagined Daniel before me... His intense blue eyes met mine, then he kissed me sweetly as he slowly slid his hands under my lacy bra, between my breasts. I felt the most delicious shivers traveling up and down my spine.

– Have you finished? Are you wearing a skirt as well?

– Yes.

– And stockings?

– As usual, yes.

– Put your hand on your thigh and pretend it's mine. Now gently glide your hand up the length of your leg, slide it under your skirt, then slip your fingers under the tops of your stockings and lightly scratch the skin underneath.

I did exactly what he said. I closed my eyes. I had the sensation that I was being lovingly embraced by a gentle sphere of warmth. I could feel his hand unbuttoning my skirt and then pushing me to stand up so that the garment could drop to the floor. I sat back down on the sofa, nearly naked now, with the phone cradled between my chin and shoulder, waiting for the next step.

– Andrea, are you there?

– I'm... I'm here... I just slipped my skirt off. I have nothing on now except for my stockings, my bra, and the skimpiest little panties that are getting so hot and moist now...

– Wait, I'm taking my pants off now... Andrea, I'm so hard... I'm enormous. I'm ready for you now. Take your bra off. Squeeze your nipples. I want them to get hard and swollen. I want to feel them getting taut under my fingertips. Go on... Do it.

I didn't need to pinch my nipples. They were already stiff with arousal and pointing towards the sky like an offering.

– Andrea, I can see them. I can feel them in my mouth... They're delicious! Pull the crotch of your panties to one side. Show me what I've been dreaming of for so long now. Spread your lips... imagine my tongue running up the inside of your thigh and then getting lost inside of you...

– Oh, Daniel... I'm so hot, I want you so much. Put down the phone right now and come to me. I'm so hot and wet. I can't stop my fingers from going down there... I'm going to let them relieve me while I wait for you...

– No, Andrea, you promised! This is part of the game. You can get dressed now. I just wanted to see if you were ready. You can go to sleep now and tomorrow I promise you won't regret the wait.

– Daniel, you're joking! I know I promised, but this is no fun at all!

– Go on, do it for me. Please. It will only make it that

much better tomorrow. Sweet dreams...

Then he hung up. I was panting, my throat was dry and my pussy was burning with arousal. He expected me to just stop! I kept repeating the old adage "absence makes the heart grow fonder" until it haunted my thoughts like a bad commercial jingle...

* * *

At last, the big day... I spent the entire morning and afternoon in an altered state. The hours crawled by at an unbearable rate. The clock hands that inched painfully forward increased the skin crawling agitation I felt as I worried continually about what I would wear that night. Tiny shivers of anxious anticipation rushed over me whenever I thought of Daniel. The only thing he had told me that morning when he had arranged our meeting for tonight was that he wanted me to wear my sexiest underwear. What I would wear over top of these undergarments would apparently be inconsequential, because they wouldn't be on me for long!

When I came home, I decided to wear my lace body suit, the one that pushed my breasts up nice and high in a charmingly exaggerated fashion. It looked more like a corset than anything else. It was made of black satin, embroidered with tiny pearls, and was fitted with solid half cups that supported my full, firm breasts. It also gave me a nice slim line... It was high cut with a lacy little crotch strip that was easily detachable... I didn't look half bad... The black stocking borders were a nice addition to the thigh high boots whose heels, although not extremely high, gave my body a nice provocative tilt. The entire effect was more than satisfactory.

The meeting place he had chosen was a trendy little downtown bar. I would have hoped for something a little more intimate but he was in charge of the evening...

He was right on time and beautifully dressed in a smart cream coloured suit. I detected the fragrance of my favourite cologne as he lowered his freshly shaven face and kissed me passionately

– You look amazing!

– Wait until you see what's underneath...

– Do you want another drink?

– Will I be needing one?

– It depends how you're feeling...

– Me or my body?

– Both...

– No problem on either score!

We got into a taxi right away. Daniel's eyes were sparkling. He gave the driver the address, took me in his arms and kissed me with startling passion. When he noticed my stockings and boots, he sucked in his breath.

– You followed my instructions to the letter... My God, I want you so much!

I felt his hand slip under my dress... The fine lace panties that covered my moist, impatient pussy suddenly became a frustration, an annoying barrier between us... His cock began to harden under my deft fingers and I was delighted to feel it attaining mouth watering proportions.

I quivered as he slid a finger between my thighs.

– Well, should we stay here, or go somewhere else?

– It won't be much longer.

I certainly hoped not... If we kept going at this rate, the cab driver might not be too happy with the big wet stain he would later find on the back seat. We were now driving through an area that was unfamiliar to me. It was the city's "Red Light" district. Prostitutes paced the sidewalks. The streets were lined from one end to the other with bars and porno theaters that streamed by us in a garish neon haze. Uneasiness began to intrude on my desire, but Daniel was quick to reassure me.

– Don't worry... I'm not going to bring you into one of those dives and I didn't hire the services of a "professional" for the evening either.

– Thank you...

We drove into a small, badly lit alleyway. Where the hell was he taking us, I wondered, feeling vaguely uneasy again? We were now several streets down from the main strip, away from all the bars and soliciting. The driver stopped the car at last in front of an alleyway door on which there was a discreet little sign that read: "by appointment only".

Daniel paid the cab fare and then helped me out of the car. We opened the door which led into a large front hallway that was practically wall to wall mirrors. No one was around... An assortment of carnival masks, of every shape, colour and variety, were hung up on the wall straight in front of us. They formed a circular pattern around another closed door. Some were decorated with lace and sequins while others were very plain. All of them were designed to cover the entire face, except for the mouth and chin.

With a smile of tender reassurance, Daniel asked me to chose two of the masks. I did so, and then he gently placed one of them over my face before putting one on himself. He opened the second door and led me towards a counter that could have been the reception desk for an upscale downtown hotel. The hotel manager (was that what he was?) in a smoking jacket welcomed us with a polite nod and a discreet little smile.

– Your names please?

– John and Mary.

– If you would like to follow me...

John and Mary? But what was this all about? My curiosity was piqued to the maximum and my nervousness increased just a touch. And these masks? Hum... My mouth was beginning to water in spite of the creeping uncertainty. Our host guided us down a long corridor which was modestly decorated with pastel coloured canvases. Was this a hotel? A restaurant? I hadn't the slightest idea... He brought us into a large, circular, high ceilinged room with appropriately subdued lighting.

The walls seemed to be covered with glass panels – or was it mirrors? Our images were somewhat reflected as we walked in but whatever it was looked too dark to be mirrors. On the other hand, there was no exterior light filtering in so I figured it surely couldn't be glass either... We looked around ourselves in amazement while the man who had accompanied us disappeared without a word. There was an enormous bed that was circular like the room and sat like a throne right in the middle of the floor. There were also some large, comfortable arm chairs that sat against the "mirrors".

Daniel seemed to be just as surprised as I was by all of this...

– It's exactly the way they described it to me, he said, only better...

– But it's so strange... Is it a hotel?

– If you like, with a few subtle differences...

– Come.

At last... I threw myself into his arms and we kissed every

bit as passionately as we had in the taxi, if not more so. As he began searching for the quickest way to get me out of my dress, the lighting in the room suddenly dimmed a touch. I looked at the panels and realized that what I had initially thought were mirrors, were actually windows. But these windows didn't lead outside... No way! This circular room was in fact the center stage in some kind of amphitheater, and I could now see groups of masked spectators surrounding us in the two levels of theater boxes – there were at least 30 – outside of here. They were shadowy figures, to be sure, but I could tell there were a lot of them. Some were alone and some were in couples and all of them were obviously there to witness our frolics. The lighting shot up again at that moment so I was prevented from getting a really good look at our audience but I had the impression that most of them, apart from the couples, were male. Everyone was poised and waiting for the show to begin.

I could tell that Daniel was trying to glean my reaction to everything from under his mask. He seemed suddenly a lot less sure of himself. I needed to convey to him that this theater, this decor, was simply perfect, an unbelievable turn-on... I grabbed his hand, kissed it tenderly and then guided it under my dress so that he could see, and feel for himself, the effect all of this was having on me. Then I took a few steps back and slowly removed my dress, flashing him my warmest smile so that he would understand how well he had succeeded in materializing a fantasy that was in fact beyond my wildest dreams. I walked slowly around the bed to make sure that every spectator could get a good look at what I had been hiding underneath my dress. I was voluptuously savouring my own provocativeness, the complete eroticism of the situation...

I was still in a kind of shock, but at this moment I felt completely, luxuriously fulfilled. I still couldn't quite believe what was happening, but I was going to linger over every instant of triumph as much as possible. I went over to Daniel and embraced him with all the passion I felt welling up inside of me. I slid my thigh between his legs so I could delight in the feel of his delectable erection. I started unbuttoning his shirt and then, with a teasing, triumphant little smile, proceeded to remove every piece of his clothing. Then I told him he had to stay put and not move as I went and lay down alone on the bed.

– And now I'm going to continue what you made me stop doing last night, you naughty little tease...

To my great surprise – and I must say, to my great satisfaction – the room began to spin very slowly. With a barely perceptible motion, the circular floor was now turning so that every spectator in the place could take in the view from all angles. With languid, cat-like sensuality I stretched myself across the bed, spreading my wickedly booted legs as far apart as possible. At least fifty pairs of turned-on eyes were observing my every move. At least twenty cocks were getting good and hard right at this moment in anticipation of the show I was about to perform. This very thought caused my pussy to flower wide open and spill its juices onto the pink satin bed sheets. I freed my breasts from the restraining corset, letting them breathe and swell with pride. I stroked them momentarily and then both hands went irresistibly between my legs... With one hand I spread those moist lips apart so that a finger from the other hand could easily reach that little parcel of flesh that can make me come instantly if I so desire...

Daniel was allowing me to experience something I

thought I could only dream about. I felt at once like an untouchable goddess of desire, and also like the lowest of whores. I imagined all those people out there breathing heavily because of what I was doing. I visualized couples fondling and making love behind those windows, so excited were they by the sight of my body, which was now inflamed with arousal. I felt irresistible.

Daniel came and joined me at the foot of the bed where he buried his face between my burning thighs. He lapped me up, bathed me in saliva, penetrated me with his tongue and fingers. I couldn't tell where the liquid flowed from anymore... The only thing I was aware of was the huge, rapidly building orgasm that would break at any second now. Daniel brought me to the brink of coming and then abruptly got up. He went to the top of the bed and grabbed both my wrists, pinning them above my head with one hand so that there was no way I could give myself the orgasmic release I so desperately needed. With his free hand he began softly stroking my throat...

He kissed my shoulders and breasts with unbearable gentleness. My skin tingled as if a million tiny electric shocks, sparks of pleasure, were running over it. Then he began lightly stroking me with his fingertips, gently at first and then more insistently. To my immense relief, he finally got back onto the bed and returned to his unfinished business, knowing full well I was going to explode any second now and not wanting any audience member to be deprived of the visual treat. I felt the waves coursing through my entire body as I came with shuddering intensity under his mouth. My belly contracted interminably, my body was writhing against my will and then, in the middle of it all, Daniel finally thrust himself inside of me.

He threw my legs over his shoulders and rode me in a frenzy. Then he turned me over, pulled me to the edge of the bed and stood behind me.

– Are you OK?

– Oh, Daniel, it's unbelievable... How did you know?

– I'll tell you someday...

At this, he grasped my hips as hard as he could and pulled me towards him, shoving himself as far inside of me as he could get. He reached a hand underneath my body and found my still engorged clitoris, which he fingered so expertly, I was reeling out of my mind once more. I was less conscious now of the people watching us, but the awareness I still had of them increased my pleasure immeasurably. In an attempt to thank them for the honour they were doing me, I secretly dedicated each of Daniel's thrusts to one of my anonymous admirers. Daniel shuddered inside of me... He felt enormous. He flipped me over onto my back and drove himself into me again, proceeding to ply my body into a series of different positions, taking me from every angle he could dream up... from the front, the back, underneath, sideways and beyond... When he finally allowed me to push him onto his back and straddle him, I used every technique I knew to please him. I sat on top of him, stroking my clitoris good and hard as I worked myself into another climax. He held up his arms so I could grasp them for support as I slowly slid myself up and down on his cock, clutching it firmly with my pussy. I sped up the motion and his expression became incredulous. I put everything I had into making love with him at that moment, all the knowledge, love, gratitude and tenderness I had in me. "Oh my baby, my love!", I cried out as I sped up faster and faster until we both came, Daniel throwing me onto my side just to give me a few ultimate thrusts...

Then the room was plunged into darkness. Lovely darkness! As much as I had appreciated the setting that had been created for us, I wanted the intimacy of darkness for this special moment that signaled the end of our first lovemaking experience. One of my most powerful fantasies had come to life and I was feeling just a little confused. Was it really me who had put on a show like that? I could barely believe it now and a flood of contradictory emotions overtook me. Daniel had given me something I had only dreamed of, but I was not certain I would ever want to do it again. The whole experience had been so intense, so incredibly mind-blowing that I was suddenly a little nervous about the whole thing. But the doubt could not cut through my euphoria... I was completely happy at this moment: amazed, fulfilled and in love, and I would not have wanted to share this moment with anyone else but Daniel...

Daniel cradled me in his arms and stroked my hair, and there was no doubt at that moment that I wanted to be in those arms for a long, long time...

– You know, we could switch places... We could go behind the glass...

– No, no... It wouldn't be the same thing. Daniel, it was... I don't know how to express it. I've been dreaming of something like that for years. Not in that kind of detail of course, but something just as perfect. It was perfect! I'm so happy I got the chance to experience the fantasy once... How about you, did you find it hard to do at all?

– Not at all. It was a little uncomfortable at the beginning, to be sure, but then it felt just fine... Stay in my arms and rest for a bit, then I'll take you on a tour. I have another surprise for you... By the way, do you want to spend the night with me?

– As if you had to ask me!

We lay there in each other's arms, both of us in the same deeply satisfied state. All at once, I experienced an intense desire to go home. We weren't going to spend the night here so there was no point in prolonging our stay too much, and he had mentioned another surprise...

I followed Daniel into a little side room where we got dressed and tidied ourselves up a little. He asked me to keep the mask on, however, and I didn't resist...

– How did you know about this place? Who thought this up?

– That's part of the surprise... Would you like the grand tour now?

– OK, but can we go back to your place soon?

– Sure. It won't take long, I promise.

He led me down another corridor and then up a flight of stairs. We came to a circular corridor down which we could see numerous doors. These doors led into the theater boxes that had housed our audience members.

– Daniel, I don't feel like watching another couple...

– Shush! Follow me.

He opened one of the doors and before I had time to say a thing, he flicked on a switch and the box was flooded with light. A man and woman, both masked, were standing inside with their arms around each other's waists.

Mannequins...

We went to the next box and Daniel repeated the same process; we found two more mannequins dressed in evening wear, gloves and a mask...

– This space belongs to a friend of mine who's a clothing designer. He uses it to show clients his new collections. That way he doesn't have to pay real models. Are you disappointed?

I had to fight hard to contain the hysterical laughter that rose to escape from me. I swallowed hard several times before answering:

I think we've completely succeeded in making this one unforgettable evening...

Midwinter Reverie

Bzzzz! Bzzzz!

Michele was dragged out of a deep sleep by the doorbell's insistent buzzing. It was only eight thirty on the first day off she had allowed herself in three weeks. Since her husband was away on a shoot outside the city for a few days, she could have easily slept in...

Bzzzz! Bzzzz! Bzzzz!

The intrusion was outrageously annoying. "Why can't the world leave me in peace for just one day!", she wailed in complete exasperation. She was now in a filthy mood and the day had only just begun. Having no other choice, she forced herself up with a huge sigh of self-pity...

She pulled on her bathrobe, left the room and descended the staircase, grumbling miserably the whole way. Through the little window beside the front door, she spied an enormous bouquet of white lilies nearly concealing the head of the young man who was delivering them.

– What? Who? Martin?

She opened the door.

– Mrs. Blake?

– Yes...

– These are for you! Have a nice day!

The flowers were magnificent but the name of the florist was nowhere to be found. Michele shrugged her shoulders, thinking the omission was rather strange... She noticed a tiny envelope stuck to the transparent plastic wrapping and guessed what was inside before she even opened it: one of those bland little cards illustrated with flowers, ribbons and little birds. She would bet any money that the card contained an uninspired little message scribbled in by some employee: "I love you, Martin". In spite of these thoughts, she still felt somewhat placated by the gift, and of course she was curious...

It was no doubt another attempt on the part of her dear husband to reconcile with her... An unimaginative and predictable effort that would certainly not solve their problems, but it was an effort nonetheless. She would have appreciated a more original approach, but this sort of gesture was typical of the man she had married and secretly hoped would change over time. She remembered the old joke she had heard once long ago: "the main problem with marriage is that the woman gets married in the hopes that her man will change and the man gets married hoping the woman won't..."

She finally detached the card. It was certainly small, but there was no design on it; it was completely white. She opened it up and found not the predictable "I love you, Martin" but an enigmatic little message that read: "I've been watching you for some time now". That was it... No signature, no initials, no "I love you" or "Forgive me". "What does that mean?", she asked herself in complete bewilderment, "I've been watching you for some time now"? This wasn't Martin's usual terse, almost abrupt style and it certainly wasn't his "too neat" handwriting either, which confirmed her premise that the message was probably dictated over the phone. But why was he suddenly being so mysterious?

The whole situation completely baffled her and she stood

by the door for quite some time puzzling over the mystery. Since she was fully awake now, there was no point going back to bed. She regretfully abandoned her plans for a lovely sleep-in and opted for the consolation of a nice hot bath instead.

The note contained in the card kept haunting her even as she stepped into a bathtub brimming with bubbles. When Martin had left the day before, the atmosphere had been pretty morose. The tension that had been building between the couple for a number of months now had finally erupted into outright quarreling and aggression. And why? She wasn't really sure... It was probably the result of accumulated grievances that should have been aired long ago but had instead been suppressed, swallowed, stuffed down... Married for five years now, they both had careers they loved but took up a lot of their time, so there were still no children. Things had been reasonably stable until quite recently though. Michele suddenly realized she couldn't remember the last time they had made love... It must have been about three months ago; just another one of those unfocused, almost mechanical endeavors, quickly expedited and pretty much devoid of passion. "And I guess that's supposed to be my fault too!", she fumed, "Because I work too much... Of course the man of the house cannot possibly be blamed for his dear wife's dissatisfaction. His work takes up a lot of his time and energy as well but it's too important to sacrifice and... My work doesn't really matter as much, does it? The least I could do is find the energy to work sixty hours a week, solve all the little household problems, and last but not least, revive the love and ardor of my warrior king. What could be simpler?"

That morning, a few days ago, everything had finally

exploded. He had told her in no uncertain terms that he was at his wits end with her. And she, with even less tact, had admitted that he didn't even excite her anymore. He had left then, and she had not heard from him since, except for this morning's little demonstration. But the words he had used... Were they proof of his desire – something she had failed to perceive of late – to persevere with their relationship? Or was he making a gesture to counteract her accusation that he didn't appreciate her? She had no idea, it just didn't make any sense. Her husband hated lack of clarity or candor in any situation. He would often blurt out: "Say what you feel and then we'll be done with it!"

"Well then", she had to ask herself, "why is he being so strange and enigmatic all of a sudden?"

The riddle was starting to consume Michele, slowly but surely. She tried telling herself that she had better things to do than spend precious time worrying about Martin's state of mind, but she couldn't stop her brain from running in circles over the problem... It was now ten thirty and her bath had done nothing to relax her. She began to pace like a lion in a cage, and then, just to add to her tension, the telephone began to ring...

It was Martin. His voice was soft, almost a murmur. Martin, who had a habit of bluntly stating the purpose of his call and then hanging up almost too abruptly, was suddenly acting unsure of himself. After the usual, pointless small talk, he finally took the plunge:

– Michele, we have to talk.

He took a long deep breath, hesitated for a second, and then began again:

– I can't concentrate... I miss you. I don't want to lose you. I'm afraid...

She was so astounded by this unexpected display of emotion, that all the hostility she had felt towards him pretty much dissolved on the spot. She tried to soften her tone, the way he had.

– Martin, I'm scared too. What's happening to us? Tell me, when did we stop talking to each other, and understanding each other? When did all of that change?

– I'm going to try and come back sooner, OK? Today is Wednesday and I know we're supposed to be shooting until next Thursday but I'm going to do everything I can to wrap it up earlier. I can't live like this anymore, always wondering whether or not you'll be there when I get back...

– Of course I'll still be here. We'll just have to take some time to really talk heart to heart.

– OK. I love you and I'll keep you posted. Take care of yourself. Promise me?

– It's a promise. Oh! I nearly forgot. Thanks.

– For what?

– You know... I got them today.

– What are you talking about?

– Come on! The flowers of course.

– What flowers? I never sent any flowers!

There was no mistaking his tone; he was sincerely surprised.

– OK, if you say so...

– No, what do you mean? What flowers?

There was a pause and then he coldly continued:

– You have an admirer?

– Of course not! It must be Lisa or David. They know things haven't been going so great these days.

– Are you keeping something from me?

– No! Listen, I have to go now. You'll call me?

– Yes I will. Talk to you soon.

He really seemed serious about not knowing anything about that bouquet... But who else would have sent her those flowers? And that strange little message? Their best friends, David and Lisa, were not aware of their problems. Martin was not the type to play these kinds of little games and it was certainly unlike him to discuss their marital problems with others.

She was more obsessed than ever with the situation. Her conscience was bothering her too. She remembered the harsh words that had been flung back and forth as Martin was leaving, and she now felt true remorse. During that last phone conversation, his desire to patch things up had seemed really sincere. She would make an effort too. Everything had been going so well up until... Up until when exactly? She had been madly in love with this man. And then the passion had slowly metamorphosed into something more down to earth. Something deeper. Yes, she knew she still loved him, and he still attracted her in spite of what she had pretended. But then... His lack of sexual interest in her was extremely hurtful and frustrating. Sex... It used to dissolve the tension and bring them together. It used to put all their petty little problems into perspective and, God knows, she missed it!

She was now far too unsettled to just stay home all day the way she had planned, although she knew she needed the rest, and tomorrow she'd be back at work again. She decided to go out after one more cup of coffee, which she'd drink in her favorite armchair, the morning paper spread out on the table before her.

It was at that point that she finally allowed herself – with considerable discomfort – to consider another possibility she hadn't dared to look at before. What if, as Martin had suggested, she did have an admirer? Some timid man who had been watching her from afar, who was now incapable of keeping his feelings for her locked away any longer... "I mean, hey, I'm not bad looking! Just because my husband doesn't seem to desire me any more..."

Michele let herself drift into reverie. Comfortably ensconced in her armchair, she began to replay the fantasy she had been entertaining since adolescence... Walking by herself along a deserted path, on a summer's night... The stranger moving slowly towards her. She hadn't seen him and had no idea he was there because he was careful to keep his footsteps synchronized with hers. Tall and thin with short, dark brown hair, he wore loose fitting faded jeans and a white shirt. His wild eyes stared rapaciously at her back, shoulders and legs. His bare feet sunk faster and faster into the moist dirt as he increased his walking speed to finally overtake her...

It was too late to run when she finally realized he was there. His arm was wrapped around her throat and a hand covered her mouth... He dragged her effortlessly into the bushes running along the path where they would be safe from discovery, then pushed her body against the trunk of an old tree. Her dress ripped on contact with the rough, dried tree bark that sank painfully into the soft flesh of her breasts. Her arms were soon being solidly attached to one of the branches, and all the while, not a word, not a threat was uttered... She could feel his penis pressing against the small of her back. He was huge, and as hard as the trunk she was tied to.

Michele was so transported by her fantasy that she barely realized she had started gently fondling her breasts, belly and thighs... The stranger brought his mouth to her ear and whispered a warning that he would have to gag her if she cried out. There wasn't anybody to hear her anyway... He yanked up her dainty little dress and ripped off her panties in one go. Down in her lower belly, she felt that familiar pressure beginning to build. It was half pain and half pleasure, a heavy warmth that spread wetly downwards while delicious little shivers traveled over her entire body.

In a daze, Michele pulled off the cumbersome dressing gown as her imaginary lover lifted her by the hips, forcing her to stand right up on tiptoe. Brutally spreading her thighs apart, he began roughly kissing her on the back of her neck, biting her shoulders and rubbing her with his stubbly chin.

Dizzy with arousal now, Michele reached one hand between her legs as the fantasy man shoved himself inside of her with all his brutal strength. He continued to bite her, muttering words that were urgent but unintelligible. There was a look of feverish agitation in his eyes as he ripped the top of her dress apart and grabbed both of her soft white breasts. His cock was plunging in and out of her with a terrible urgency.

Stunned by the intensity of this fantasy, Michele began frantically rubbing her swollen pussy. Her fingers knew how to conquer all of those tender areas by heart, and they pursued their goal with a vengeance, massaging the moist pink flesh, then disappearing inside of that hot wet opening... until she came.

* * *

It was already noon when she arrived at her office looking a little haggard. Sonia, her faithful assistant, seemed stupefied to see her. After quickly explaining that she simply had too much work to just stay at home, Michele grabbed up her mail and headed for her office. The mail consisted of the usual stuff: Christmas cards, bills that always came too early and advertisement pamphlets. But there was also a plain white envelope with no return address on which only her name was written. That writing... She was sure it was the same writing she had found on the tiny card that had come with the flowers this morning!

As she ripped open the card, she was both excited and curious. On a plain white sheet of paper was written: "My dearest Michele, I hope the flowers pleased you. I am watching you and wanting you. I can't wait forever."

Once again, there were no initials or signature. Nothing... And it wasn't Martin's writing, she was certain of that. She went to Sonia's office immediately.

– Tell me something, Sonia, she asked her, how did this envelope arrive?

– I don't know... As a matter of fact, it was on the ground when I arrived, as if someone had slipped it under the door. One thing I do know: it wasn't delivered in person. I would remember...

Sonia suddenly looked concerned.

– Why, is something wrong?

– No, no. Nothing's wrong. It's just a little strange that's all.

She returned to her desk and shoved the envelope into her bag so she could take it home and compare it to the writing on the other card.

That evening, as she compared both envelopes, she could see that the writing was identical...

* * *

Thursday, eleven thirty.

Michele tried to work but her heart wasn't in it. Her office was a real mess and she had been putting off the reorganization date since the fall. Making an instant decision to rectify the situation, she immediately called Sonia in to help her. Only when Sonia closed the door to Michele's office, did they both see the parcel resting against the wall.

Michele was certain she had never seen this box before. It was white and rectangular, a typical department store box, but there was nothing to indicate who might have sent it. She unwrapped it nervously and stared at the contents open-mouthed... Two magnificent lilies had been placed over the tissue paper. She hesitated a second or two before lifting the paper with slightly trembling hands. Carefully folded in this anonymous box was a superb white lace negligee with delicately embroidered trimming and tiny satin straps. And, as she suspected, there was a little white card sitting at the bottom of the box. But this time, the only message written was: "Soon, my love." Nothing more.

Sonia had a knowing little smile on her face but Michele was totally perplexed once more. How had this package arrived at her office? This whole situation was becoming a slightly disturbing treasure hunt. If her husband was responsible for this puzzle, then the only plausible explanation was that he wasn't out of the city after all. But why so much mystery? This was not the kind of thing that would usually amuse him at all. But if it wasn't him, then someone else was waiting in the wings. "I'm stumped by this!", she thought to herself, "I'm not the heroine of some soap opera. I'm Michele Blake, an ordinary woman married to an ordinary man, leading an ordinary life. It's just that my husband got it into his head to try something a little different, that's all". But she didn't really manage to convince herself of this...

– Hum... Your husband has good taste.

Sonia's expression was mischievous, and even, Michele thought, a little envious. She gave her boss a sly little wink and then both of them got back to work and forgot the incident.

As soon as Michele arrived home that evening, she slipped on her present. It suited her to perfection. Martin – she was now convinced it could only be him – knew her body better than she thought... This negligee was sublimely feminine, soft and light. For the first time in ages, she felt sensual, almost desirable. She was extremely curious to see where this little game would lead, and fully intended to play her part to the end. Martin had left no number where she could reach him, so Michele had no choice but to wait impatiently for his call.

But the telephone didn't ring once all night.

The next day was Friday and nothing unusual happened. There were no parcels or phone calls, and no surprises to break up the monotony of the day. She was a little disappointed. She had been wondering what Martin's next move might be, and she had to admit that she was starting to find the special attention exciting. Had he thrown in the towel already?

She had no desire to go out that night, so she spent the evening at home. After a lovely meal complemented by a fine glass of wine, Michele simply allowed herself to drift into the pleasure of being alone. She adored this cozy feeling of intimacy, independence and freedom. Looking out the window, she could see lazy snow flakes floating about. Everything was calm and still: a perfect winter's scene. The outside noises were muffled by the thick snow that had been accumulating since the beginning of the day. The wine was making her feel very relaxed and she decided to put her negligee back on... But something was missing. She put on some music to suit the mood and then, to her great pleasure, her imaginary lover returned to haunt her... Always the same man, the same dream lover she had created so long ago. He came up behind her and wrapped his arm around her neck the way he always did, but this time he was right there in her home. In one brutal yank, a fisted hand ripped the negligee from her body, the same merciless hand that threw her face down onto a pile of cushions. He threw himself on top of her and pinned her to the spot, immediately raising her pelvis with the help of nearby cushions. And then, with no prelude at all, he invaded her with his fingers and tongue. The rough skin of his hand chafed that most tender region of her body and the famished mouth devoured her. The pain was exquisite, the fear delicious, and the pleasure unbearable... and then he stopped abruptly and got to his knees... Pulling his jeans down around his thighs, he drove his member brutally inside of her, tearing and bruising her delicate flesh. The furious thrusting got deeper and harder as he slid in and out of her pleasure-wet pussy with ease. He was huge and she felt the tender skin of her lips stinging under the assault. He knew he was causing her pain and enjoyed every second of it. Tearing into her, he grunted quietly as he drove his cock faster and faster until she exploded with pleasure. That night, her body once more swathed in satin and lace, Michele fell asleep with no trouble at all.

Saturday morning she was awakened by the phone. It was Martin.

– Hi. Am I waking you?

– Yes, but that's OK. How are you?

– Not bad. The shoot's going well and I think I'll be able to come back on Monday. Have you thought about us? I really miss you, Michele.

She said nothing, so he continued:

– I was wrong. I wish I had never said those things to you.

– Me too, Martin, I'm really sorry. But we're going to have to really talk if we want this thing to work out. That would be great if you came back Monday...

And then, with a tiny note of sarcasm she added:

– So... The shoot's going well, is it?

– Yes, it's going fine. Listen, I can't wait much longer, I...

His breathing was eloquent to her.

– I want you.

When was the last time he had said anything like that to her? He had to be the "secret admirer", she was certain of it now.

– I want you too...

And then she tried to make him open up by saying:

– And if you could see me now, you wouldn't be able to hold yourself back...

– Yes, I can picture you right now in your cute little night gown... Don't say anymore, it's hard enough as it is!

– OK, if that's the way you want to play it... Good night my love.

– Bye. See you Monday.

Nothing more. He had made no allusion at all to her new outfit, at least nothing conclusive. He was stronger than she thought. She had to admit that for the time being, he was leading the game. But she certainly wasn't going to let that be the case for much longer.

It was close to ten o'clock when she arrived at the office. She liked working on Saturdays; the place was always calm and deserted, and the telephone, except for her own personal line, was hooked up to the answering machine. She went to work immediately and didn't stop until almost three o'clock when hunger took over. A sandwich at the little corner restaurant would solve her problem, and it made her mouth water just to think about it. Her personal telephone began to ring just as she was about to leave.

– Hello?

– Michele.

– Yes. Who is it?

– I'm watching you.

A hoarse, low-pitched voice and heavy breathing... It wasn't Martin's voice. A truly unpleasant shiver gathered force inside of her and rushed up her spine.

– Who is it?

No answer, only heavy breathing

– If that's you Martin, stop your little game. You've won, OK? You've outdone me.

– So, Martin must be your husband's name? Tell me Michele, does he look at you the same way I do? Does he desire you as much as I do?

– OK, that's enough. I'm hanging up. This isn't funny anymore, Martin.

– Martin should have seen you last night. That little negligee I gave you really suits you. I like white. It's so pure, soft and gentle. But you don't like men who are too gentle, do you Michele? I'm kind of the opposite of that myself, and I can give you what you've been dreaming of for so long now...

Her heart nearly stopped beating. She was frozen on the spot. Last night? Last night?

– Don't be afraid Michele, I don't wish you any harm. You excite me Michele. When you touch yourself the way you did last night, I get unbelievably turned on. If I even think of you, I get so big and hard that even you wouldn't be able to handle it. I want to watch you come. You've never had a man touch you the way you'd like, huh Michele? You deserve better...

CLIC!

She had certainly had enough of this now! Her hunger had vanished and the only thing she wanted to do right at that moment was get the hell out of there as fast as possible. If it was Martin, he was definitely going too far. She wondered what he had been up to for three days! Had he been watching her? And why didn't he come to sleep at the house if he wasn't shooting? This little game was definitely not fun anymore. "And if it's not him", she wondered with increasing alarm, "then what"? It meant she certainly wasn't safe. Not at all... She turned to look out of the window and saw that the light morning snow fall had turned into a storm. Not again! Well, she could forget the sandwich. She decided to go home and lock herself there until tomorrow. If Martin called her tonight, she was going to tell him loud and clear that he was going just a little too far. Seeing how anxious she was, he would surely abandon the game. If he denied everything and insisted it wasn't him, she would call the police.

She was feeling better already as she left the building. But what a snow storm there was now! She listened to the car radio as the newscasters strongly suggested that people go home before the weather situation worsened. They predicted the wind would lift and that twenty five to thirty centimeters of snow would fall before the morning. "What a shit storm!", she thought to herself. She actually loved the snow, but this was the third storm in two weeks! No one needed to convince her to return home. She ran a few errands on the way, through traffic that was getting worse by the minute. Night was falling, and it was with great relief that she finally parked the car in front of the house...

Waiting on the doorstep, almost buried in the snow, was another bouquet of half frozen white lilies. She hurried inside, tore open the inevitable little envelope and checked the card which read: "Sorry I frightened you Michele. I don't want to scare you. I just want to possess you. Once, just once. You mustn't be afraid of your fantasies..."

Ah! There you go! Relief after fear. She clearly remembered now that Martin had once reproached her for not sharing her fantasies. He said it was normal and healthy to have them and that if she just talked about them openly, it would give him some idea of how to please her better. But there were some things that Michele just considered too personal and her fantasy life was one of them. Martin was a gentle, patient man, and that's why she loved him. But one day, he had been so insistent about hearing her fantasies that she had decided, in the hopes of avoiding an argument, to try and state her point of view. She had simply explained:

"What if, say, one of my fantasies involved being "attacked" by a stranger. That could end up troubling you because you're a gentle person and you might wonder why I loved "you" and not someone more aggressive. You might also think I was a bit strange. Most women fear rape, but some women do eroticize it in a perverse sort of way. I think some fantasies should remain secret. Would it really be exciting to be attacked by a stranger? No. And what would be the point in talking about it anyway? It would just make me uncomfortable, and would totally confuse you. That's it, let's drop the subject, OK?"

He seemed to accept her point of view and never broached the subject again. She didn't know how to tell him that all she wanted was for him to be a little bit more aggressive in bed sometimes. Stronger, more passionate, more brutal...

Except that... Michele was having trouble believing that her husband, who liked to think of himself as "correct" and conservative, could display this much imagination. At this point, she was desperate to believe he was capable of it, but the troubling doubts still persisted. This kind of behavior was so unlike the Martin she had known for so long! He would never get it into his head to do something so unpredictable, so "sexual". Not her Martin. But then, who could it be?...

The storm raged down in all it's terrifying splendor, one of those storms you can only see in this part of the world, and not every year either! The whole works were supposed to come down during the course of the next few hours: snow, hail, freezing rain, thunder, lightning... all complemented by hurricane-like winds. Michele wouldn't have wanted to be anywhere else right now but here at home. She was happy here, all bundled up in her nice warm dressing gown. But a storm this violent always made her nervous. Excited, but uneasy at the same time. She might have trouble sleeping. Nothing a little glass of wine couldn't cure, of course. It would at least calm her down.

Hours went by and Martin never phoned. She finally gave up on hearing from him and went to bed.

She had been deeply asleep when someone grabbed her

hair with seemingly superhuman force and a gloved hand clamped over her mouth. Michele thought she would die of fright. After the initial flood of adrenaline, her terrified heart started up slowly again and then began pounding so frantically she thought it might smash through her chest. Her thoughts flew wildly as she tried to grasp what was happening. A dream couldn't be this realistic! When she finally understood that it wasn't a dream, she tried to scream at the top of her lungs, but no sound emerged. Her cry stayed mute even though it ripped through her throat.

She could hardly breathe as she struggled with all her might. But the man pinned her arms down and sat firmly on her buttocks, crushing her wrists cruelly with his knees. She succeeded in giving her assailant a few good kicks but caused him not one ounce of harm. She tried in vain to calm herself down and analyze the situation. "Don't panic, don't panic!", she kept repeating to herself over and over... He suddenly spoke:

– Calm down! I don't want to hurt you. I've been looking at you for so long now... I couldn't wait any longer. Don't make me hit you... You're too beautiful, Michele. I want you now.

His tone was categorical.

It was him... Him! She tried to wriggle around and look up at him. The complete darkness of the bedroom plunged her into even greater terror, and not being able to get a look at him made her feel unbearably vulnerable. A million thoughts scurried through her brain along with questions she might never get the chance to answer: "How did he get in? Who is it? What did I do? Do I know him? Me, a rape victim? Me? Why me? Am I going to die? I don't want to die!" Even through the panic that was building up speed inside of her, she understood that the darkness was in fact a blessing. Perhaps he would do her no harm, knowing she could never recognize him. "Calm down, try to stay calm... Calm down!", she told herself furiously.

And then, as if to confirm her last thoughts, he said:

– I promise that if you stay calm, I won't do you any harm.

He tried to make his tone reassuring.

– I will leave when I've finished with you and you will never see me again, I promise.

The stranger gently stroked her hair.

– Don't worry, I love you. I'll do you no harm.

Michele could not believe her ears. This was insane. Completely insane. He loved her? But who was it? She knew him? "Oh! Martin, where are you when I really need you?"... He interrupted her thoughts by turning her brusquely onto her back. She couldn't stop herself from trying to look through the darkness at his face, but it was no use... She could only discern the shape of his head. The man didn't manage to re-restrain her on time, and she released a piercing cry and desperately attempted to hit him with her now freed fists. But the only thing she got for her efforts was the bitter taste of leather as he clapped his hand over her mouth once more.

– I told you to stay calm...

The voice. The hoarse, low-pitched voice was gone, and the one replacing it was soft, familiar and patient... Martin! But the fist pinning her wrists above her head was still just as cruel and unflinching.

– You can scream if you want but no one will hear you. No one. You're mine now. I've been waiting for much too long now. I love you. Don't resist me. I wish you no harm.

She suddenly relaxed, and he took advantage of the opportunity to quickly gag her with a silk scarf. She was still blinded by the darkness, but she knew it was Martin. Oh yes! It was him all right. It had been him since the beginning. The relief she felt made her realize the total absurdity of one of her most powerful fantasies. As relief melted fear, her pussy began to flower. She felt her lips open up and swell with desire. Martin kissed her lightly on the temple and then firmly tied her wrists together over her head. Michele was in pain... but it was as if she had been waiting for this moment all of her life, as if a door was opening up onto some sublime sense of well-being. He grabbed her nightdress and ripped it off in one shot. She shivered. She tried to get up but he grabbed her roughly by the shoulders and flattened her against the bed.

– So, you're not going to be nice about this? Well then, I have no choice...

Martin straddled her waist and slid off his belt in menacing silence. She continued to struggle and kept trying to cry out and get up, but she wasn't strong enough... He wrapped the belt through the silk scarf that restrained her wrists and then tied it solidly to one of the bed posts. She was completely trapped now... It was wonderful, delicious, and also terribly frustrating. He took hold of her panties and slid them tightly down the length of her legs, exquisitely burning her skin. The intensity of the heat she felt in her lower belly was like a revelation; a sharp but muted aching that bore down between her legs and made her wetter than she had ever been. It was a sensation she had been dreaming of forever...

– What were you doing last night all alone? You were thinking about me weren't you?

Michele detected a smile.

– Is this what you wanted? Is this what you were waiting for?

She had never in her wildest dreams thought that she would ever hear Martin talk to her like this. He seemed truly angry, impatient, and not to be defied. He lifted her pelvis with one hand and began stroking her pussy with the other. Hard, much too hard; exactly the way she wanted it. His fingers kneaded her pitilessly, the combination of pleasure and pain was almost unendurable. Her wrists were killing her and her entire body was taut and alert. But her belly was on fire and she could feel the fluid sliding down between her cheeks. She had summoned this pleasure, desired it as much as the man who was on top of her now. He became the symbol of pain and she waited for him impatiently. As if he could read her thoughts, Martin grabbed both her breasts and squeezed them hard. He raked his nails across her nipples until she was screaming inside. Lukewarm tears ran slowly down her face. Tears of joy, or tears of pain? She didn't know anymore. Her assailant then started pinching and biting her breasts, her throat, her shoulders and belly. He descended the length of her body until his teeth were murdering the oh so delicate flesh of her inner thighs while his hands continued to pinch her as hard as he could. When his teeth finally reached the wide open lips of his victim, the cry she had contained finally resounded throughout the bedroom. After awhile, her lover pulled an object she couldn't identify from his coat pocket. The scarf that was wrapped around her mouth disappeared and Martin forced the strange item into her mouth. It was hard, a good sized cylinder that was either metal or glass. Then he pulled it out abruptly and inserted it lower down, none too gently, in the place she wanted it so desperately to be. He slowly made love to her with this object so that she would be ready for his intimidating size. He shoved it in and out of her more and more rapidly and brutally until Michele felt herself on the verge of coming. Then he pulled the object out and threw it against the wall where it exploded into a million pieces.

The barely perceptible sound of his pants being unzipped with demented slowness was a torment to his prey. He knelt over her face. At last! He forced her mouth open and invaded it mercilessly with the cock she gratefully accepted. He drove his member deep down her throat, choking her and causing new tears to flow. With great difficulty, she slid her tongue around him, taking him in as best she could. It hurt, and her pussy was starved for him now. The pleasure she felt was almost frightening...

– You like this don't you? That's really too bad.

He was up in one bound. He retreated from the bed and left the room with deliberate slowness.

– Good-bye, Michele.

– What!!!!! Come back here, come back right now!

She heard the front door squeak open and a puff of cold air made it's way right back to the bedroom. He had left! What had she done to deserve this kind of abandonment? He was actually leaving her there, all tied up and panting with desire, on the verge of the most powerful orgasm of her life! The bastard! And then:

– Did you really think I'd just leave you here like this?

The brutal caresses began again. He penetrated her with his fingers as he pinched and bit her all over. Unable to hold back anymore, Michele came in spite of herself.

– I didn't give you permission to come. You weren't supposed to!

He stood stark still for one tiny instant.

– I'm going to have to punish you.

He turned her over onto her belly, lifted her pelvis and entered her, with no warning in one violent thrust. She thought she was going to tear in two. Never had Martin made love to her with such savagery, such brutality, and she loved it!

She begged him not to stop. He bent over and grabbed her breasts from behind, squeezing and scratching them as he did. He insinuated himself with ease into the deepest parts of her. She was crushed and nearly suffocated by his substantial weight and it felt like her thighs and buttocks were being split in two. She came again, and then again, but he was still harder than ever as he continued to violate her with such force that she had no choice but to completely submit under the attack... Her belly contracted and her body writhed under the violence of the orgasm that seemed to go on forever, forcing her lover to speed up and drive his shaft inside of her with even greater fury until he came as well, spraying her exhausted back, buttocks and thighs...

They were breathless, exhausted, and floating in a dreamlike lethargy. "If it was all a dream", thought Michele, "then I've truly outdone myself in the fantasy department!" Martin gently untied her wrists and lay down beside her. Her feelings were well worth analyzing, but she felt beyond words right now. She was completely and utterly fulfilled. They fell asleep together and the last thing she remembered was the vague overall throbbing of her body and the last little spasms of pleasure that had followed her to the edge of sleep.

The next morning, Michele woke up to the smell of

coffee brewing downstairs. The sun was shining and the storm had left a beautiful lace-like pattern of frost on the window. Martin, the Martin she had always known, entered the room carrying a tray containing a sumptuous breakfast. He was back to normal: a young professional in a velour bathrobe, with a voice that was soft and tender. He looked lovingly at his wife, but there was a sparkle in his eye that hadn't been there before...

He kissed her lightly on the forehead as he placed the tray in front of her. Right there beside the breakfast was a magnificent bouquet of white lilies and a little white envelope. Inside there was a card that bore an insipid little drawing of pink flowers, ribbons, and little birds. And written inside, in the familiar hand writing, was the predictable: "I love you, Martin".

METAMORPHOSIS

OR

AN ORDINARY MAN'S EXTRAORDINARY ADVENTURE

Bernard still had no idea how it had happened... and it couldn't have mattered less! The dramatic changes in him were indeed extraordinary, but so were the consequences of that change...

He did not consider the possible causes of this transformation worth studying. It would be a useless exercise anyway. The only important fact was that his lifelong dream and greatest aspiration came true from one day to the next. He was transformed, overnight it seemed, from a chubby, myopic little toad into a veritable Don Juan.

Bernard had never believed in miracles, but he had been sadly dragging his secret wish around since he was very little. His flaws, however, shouldn't be exaggerated. He hadn't been that horrible looking before. But now! It happened one fine morning, just like that. There had been no deafening peals of thunder or stupendous flashes of lighting. The hand of God did not reach down to bestow a divine blessing on his head. At least, not that he knew of...

He had gone to bed the night before around midnight, as he usually did, after drinking a few beers and numbing his brain with a few pretty vapid TV sit-coms. And the next morning, BANG! Without the least little bit of pain or any remarkable sensation for that matter, the new him had materialized...

Entering the bathroom that day to proceed with his usual early morning routine, he didn't even notice that the mirror was reflecting an altogether different face. It was only after his first coffee, when he went to shave, that he noticed the change and thought he must be dreaming: a stranger in the mirror was staring back at him with a stupefied expression on his face... A stranger who didn't have the expected swollen eyes and wild strands of hair flying all over the place, the way it was every morning. But this stranger still looked somewhat familiar... He realized it was still him, just a new, super improved version of him.

The first thing Bernard noticed was the hair. The head his hair was quickly abandoning, something he was powerless to stop, now boasted a luxurious mane that would have made Samson green with envy. And this was only the beginning. The next realization was that the hideous mustache that had partially caused his divorce was gone and the all too familiar soft, doughy contours of his face had sharpened into the most seductive planes and angles. His body seemed to have suddenly lengthened, but that was because the extra pounds that lovingly encircled his gradually expanding waistline had melted like butter in the sun. His shoulders had become god-like, practically bursting out of his sleeves. "I'll have to get bigger clothes!", he thought. His stomach had flattened and was now rippling with superb muscles, and his once hairless, lily-white chest was now thickly covered with manly chest hair. "I can go topless now!", he told himself happily. But these were still not the most extraordinary changes...

No, the most unbelievable transformation of all had taken place between his legs, the domain of the organ that had been limp and useless for ages. He stared at it now in all of its "ready for anything" glory; it had reached a size that he had only ever seen in the raunchiest porn movies...

His pointless little cock had metamorphosed into a veritable deadly weapon, a love machine, a public menace! And this missile was waiting impatiently to be fired...

The blessedly transformed Bernard dealt with the shock, pleasant as it was, as best he could and prepared himself for yet another day at the office. Questions that were crossing his mind such as: "What the hell happened?" or "Will my friends recognize me?" became irrelevant as soon as he pulled on his pants and felt his new source of pride protesting against the lack of space.

Leaving his apartment that morning – and every other morning after that – Bernard knew the true meaning of the word happiness. And every night from then on, he would recite thank-you prayers to every god he could think of. That way, the one responsible for such generosity would understand his gratitude and wouldn't abandon him.

His life had never been the same since that marvelous morning. For the first time, women, actual drop-dead-gorgeous women, were literally falling into his arms. Bernard, who had never thought in his wildest dreams he could ever attract the attention of these foxes who crossed his path every day, was getting smile after tantalizing smile.

One day as he was patiently waiting at a traffic light, some movement to the left of him caught his eye. Turning around, he saw an amazing blonde wearing lipstick that matched the shade of her little red sports car, and she was flashing him the most incredible four headlight smile. She then started blowing him moist little kisses, her voluptuous breasts rising up with each one. His joy was indescribable! "Me!", he said to himself ecstatically, "She's doing this to me!" He desperately wanted to get in her car and have her drive to some discreet little motel, but he had a rendez-vous with Cynthia, an adorable redhead he had met a few days ago.

How could he choose? Bernard found himself projected into the world of a virgin adolescent willingly locked up in a women's prison with hundreds of lust-maddened females dying to give him his first introduction to sex...

He kept wondering: "Did some kind of fairy do this to me? A fantastic fairy, with a body to make a saint risk damnation, who chose me, above all others, to be her lifelong sexual partner?" Whenever he felt any pangs of conscience for his promiscuous behavior, he just told himself: "The good fairy also has the power to remove the spell whenever she pleases, so I better take full advantage of the situation, even if it's only to perfect my technique for the day when she claims me..."

It was Cynthia whom he finally honored with his presence, and this decision proved to be anything but disappointing. She did unbelievable things to him! And since his new improved, splendidly alert organ performed with a tirelessness he just wasn't used to, he did not disappoint her either. He took her four times during that unforgettable night and by the end of it his cock, as resilient and high performance as it was, felt like it might fall off. For hours, as she completely submitted to his every demand, he used her body in as many imaginative ways as possible, making sure every orifice was carefully exploited. At one point, however, she jumped up and took the initiative. Firmly straddling him, she rode him as hard as she could and screamed with pleasure at his exceptional prowess.

He was a little tired and irritable the next morning, but ready to start all over again. And that's when his ingenious idea came to him. After a quick study of his financial situation, Bernard came to the conclusion that he could afford to treat himself to a little something. He couldn't remember the last time he had taken advantage of his single life. Of course, the old Bernard's single life had never offered him many opportunities to take advantage of, but all of that had certainly changed now... His last holiday had been spent trying to save his marriage to Janine. All that effort only to watch her walk out the door again taking the little one with her. So...

An enticing advertisement in the paper made him opt for a cruise between Miami, the Bahamas and Cuba. But a certain turn of events along the way made him miss the second part of the cruise...

The last thing he had imagined when he signed on for the trip was that the cruise ship would eventually leave him behind while he blissfully floated on a small raft off the shore of Key West, listening to the crystalline laughter of young women coming from the nearby sailboat as he continued to recover from the shock of his first encounter with Valérie, a wonderfully fascinating woman with her own special brand of sensuality...

He met Valérie on the "Sea Queen" during the first leg of the trip. She was French, but through some connection or other, she had landed a summer job working as a hostess on the ship before returning to her studies in the fall. Bernard's first days on board were spent lazing by the pool in the sun where he read thrillers and admired the dazzling sea in addition to his darkening tan. The latter was a revelation because his old skin would have reddened at first exposure. The ship was incredibly luxurious, but he barely noticed: he was surrounded by young bronzed beauties who presented him with their well-oiled bodies, graceful gestures, easy smiles, and light conversation. There wasn't much more to be said!

As he had decided to "test" his limitations to see how long he could wait before tasting one of these sumptuous dishes, Bernard was content for the moment to flash teasing little smiles at some of them and approving winks at the others. But there was one girl in particular who sent his hormones racing into delirious overdrive: Valérie. He hadn't yet had the chance to engage her in conversation, but he had certainly noticed her; it would have been impossible not to. And suddenly, there she was, sitting on the chair next to him in a fabulous white bikini that flattered her gracefully slender but also muscular body. He was blinded by her dazzling white teeth as she smiled engagingly and asked him with feigned shyness if he would mind oiling her back. Needing no persuasion, Bernard nodded his head dumbly in response.

– Vous êtes Americain?

– Uh, no. I'm from Toronto.

– Ah, Canadien.

– Yes...

– Oh! So... cute!

He wasn't sure whether she meant that he was cute or the fact that he was a Canadian... Who cared! Then he noticed her strange medallion. It was a tear-shaped pendant, about two inches long, on a solid silver chain. He asked her what it was and to his great surprise she blushed:

– Eet ees a secret...

In spite of his curiosity, Bernard was far too busy looking at her to ask any more questions... She was a wet dream come true for any man who could still get it up: tall and thin, with sensuous feline grace and silky smooth skin that was tanned to perfection, long, sun bleached hair, sparkling blue eyes and teeth that had probably made some dentist very rich... In short, the kind of woman who would have caused his ex-wife Janine, whose irrationality was almost comical, to start ranting and raving with jealousy.

Before his transformation, a woman like Valérie, even if she was just passing by in the street, would have made Bernard blush crimson and wish he could just disappear so he wouldn't have to watch her beautiful eyes coming to a rest on an old toad like him. But that was all in the past now! As he rubbed the oil onto her appetizing back with a hand that was trembling with gratitude, he was delighted to hear her suddenly blurt out:

– You are married?

That French accent made the end of his impetuous cock quiver and he lost no time in replying:

– Divorced... and how!

Her smile was a little perplexed as if she hadn't fully understood him. When Bernard repeated the phrase in the minimal French that he knew, she smiled more broadly. She told him that she was a student in Florida and that she had taken this summer job, which she loved, three years in row now to help finance her studies. She was a hostess and her job was to welcome the passengers, who were charmed by her accent, and make sure they were happy with everything. In short, she was there to do her best to make everyone's cruise as pleasant as possible. In her spare time, she solved little problems and worked on her tan. Since she knew all about the on-board activities, she reminded him that tonight was "Casino" night, which had been planned with the aim of teaching passengers how not to lose all their money the first night they arrived at the Bahamas.

She concluded her pitch with an appealing sigh, stating her hope that Bernard would be there... He was just about to deliver his enthusiastic reply when a bell sounded from somewhere and Valérie got up to answer the call.

– Je dois partir... I mean, I have to go. I will see you tonight?

– Mais oui!...

Bernard stayed by the pool for a little while longer to admire the scenery before him, but as he wanted to look sharp for that very promising evening ahead, he didn't linger. He began with a little gym session to pump up the muscles that still stunned him every time he took a look. Afterwards, a masseuse used all her expertise to make him unwind, and then he let the ship's hairdresser make sure his new mane was at its peak of perfection.

He had an early, light supper before going back to his cabin to change into something that would enhance his irresistibility that much further. Valérie was going to get the guy that had only existed in her dreams. That is, until today...

A quick phone call soon brought the florist to his door with an enormous bouquet of pink roses. He would be offering these to Valérie once he brought her back to his cabin, although he knew it was hardly necessary; by that time she would be burning with desire, already in love, and a slave to his incredible charisma. Champagne was also ordered ahead of time and carefully placed in his refrigerator. "All I have to do is whip it out at exactly the right moment, pop the cork and *voilà*!", he told himself with a greedy smile. He stood in front of the mirror in his best suit, sprinkled himself with a few drops of eau de Cologne and finally left to pursue a conquest that was already "in the bag".

He noticed her as soon as he walked into the bar. It would have been difficult, perhaps even unnatural, to not have... Valérie was wearing a white satin shift that molded the contours of her body so that her lack of underwear – or the tinyness of any existing underwear – was unmistakable. Bernard ran an impatient tongue over lips suddenly gone dry when Valérie beckoned him to come over and join her.

He managed to mumble that she was "très belle", which was the only French adjective he could come up with. She in turn told him that he was very "séduisant". Good... Everything seemed to be moving in exactly the right direction! Taking him by the arm, she asked him if he had ever been to a casino. His answer was an honest yes... (He didn't think it was necessary to include the fact that the pudgy loser he used to be had once lost two hundred dollars in less than an hour...) She was delighted! Giving him her cutest wink, she instantly concluded that there was no need for them to stay here... A light, deft little hand pulled Bernard out onto the deck and then further down until they reached the bow. The music from the various bars and restaurants was much less audible here and they were softly caressed by gentle night air that was warm and salty.

The bridge was deserted since all the evening activities had just begun. Without a word, Valérie pressed herself against him, grabbed his powerful neck and kissed him hard. All resistance would have been futile... not to mention stupid! Her satin clad knee slid between his quaking legs as she began rubbing it over his cock, which had been uncontainable since he first caught sight of her at the bar. She sighed softly in appreciation and murmured:

– Je te veux...

"What to do? What to say?" Such idiotic questions! He

kissed her until he was breathless and then tried in vain to drag her towards his cabin. Shaking her head, Valérie gestured him to follow her instead. He obeyed like a good dog following his mistress, like a good boy following his dick...

He realized that she was leading him to the spa area. It was closed at this hour and he couldn't help but ask himself what she could possibly want to do in there. She pulled out a huge set of keys from her purse, opened the door as quietly as possible and gently pushed him to the area where the whirlpools were located. Everything in this top section of the boat was closed and the new lovers were quite alone. Bernard tried to tell her that he had cold champagne in his cabin, but she was already heading purposefully towards the reception counter. Choosing another key, she opened an office door, entered the room and came out almost immediately with two glasses and a champagne bottle on ice.

After swiftly popping the cork, Valérie filled the glasses and then disappeared behind the counter. The whirlpools were suddenly activated and the hot water began to steam and swirl. To Bernard's great pleasure, she gently pushed him into a chair and began undulating her sensational body in front of him. The moonlight shining through the window seemed to dance all over her intoxicating dress. One of her hands slid behind her back and expertly unzipped the satin cocoon that contained her body, letting it drop to the floor. Wearing only her shoes and her strange medallion now, she turned around to let him admire her nicely tanned behind as she descended into the whirlpool that suddenly became irresistibly inviting. Bernard quickly shed his own clothes, trying as much as possible not to appear too eager. This was certainly not the moment to make a fool of himself by tripping up on his pants... That was something only the old Bernard would have done!

The water temperature was perfect, but Valérie wouldn't allow him to immerse himself immediately. After he had descended a few steps, her lovely little hands began lightly splashing him all over... Closing his eyes, he savored the lovely feeling and then felt her tongue timidly licking the end of his cock before her lips firmly enfolded the whole thing. He was trapped in the delicious warmth of her mouth as her tongue performed circles around his dick. Bernard wanted to stuff himself down her throat, even though it might choke her. But she wouldn't let him. Massaging his buttocks with one hand, she slid her other hand between his legs and gently clasped his enormous testicles. A little more water was trickled onto him and then Valérie made him turn around... She began licking his upper thighs, working her way up to his back, then down again to his cheeks and in between them... His knees began to buckle and he was having trouble standing.

Valérie eased herself back in front of him again, this time sliding his entire penis into her mouth. She sure knew what she was doing! Her mouth was gliding slowly up and down, up and down, squeezing him firmly, her soft warm tongue caressing him. Slender hands solidly gripped his ass and her teeth rubbed him just enough... Little cries of pleasure escaped from him now... He let her torture him this way for several minutes more without uttering one word. It gave him tremendous pleasure, and for the time being he felt no need to rush things.

It was at this moment that something started tickling his leg. He didn't pay any attention to it at first, so transported was he by the magic of Valérie's mouth. She was still massaging his ass and lightly sprinkling him with water from time to time. As she momentarily stopped, Bernard saw her licking a shiny object. He knew immediately what she intended to do... Spreading his cheeks gently apart with her left hand, her right hand slowly inserted something inside of him. He was being penetrated by the tear-shaped pendant and the surprise almost made him come on the spot. Wrapping the chain around her fingers, she slid the pendant even further inside of him, carefully retracting and inserting it while her mouth moved to the same rhythm over his cock!

Bernard was so weak in the knees now, he knew they were on the point of buckling. His pleasure was so intense that he was afraid he wouldn't be able to contain himself much longer and that he would come in spite of himself just like the old Bernard, causing him to die of shame... He focused on this thought and managed to stop his orgasm, temporarily at least. His balls were ready to explode and his entire belly was on the verge of contracting into spasms of pure ecstasy that would be more intense that he had ever imagined possible. The lips around him sped up so much, and so effectively, that he had to rip his cock away to stop himself from exploding into her mouth. This would have been just fine at another time, but right now he wanted to penetrate her, possess her, make her scream and writhe with pleasure like he had with her.

He went down to join her in the water, making her sit on one of the steps so he could get his lips to her pussy, but the hot water on his cock made him quickly realize that he wanted to be inside of her NOW! And that's just where he went. Once his cock was solidly anchored, Valérie raised herself a little so that they were both kind of half floating. They were suddenly transformed into weightless beings, which was a strange sensation combined with the feeling that he was going to come at any second... She floated on her back while Bernard knelt on the bottom of the bath, the hot water bubbles tickling him all over. He drew her closer towards him so he could impale her even more deeply and then, in spite of all his efforts, he came... It seemed to just go on and on, his deeply submerged cock thrusting further and further inside the gasping, writhing Valérie...

She agreed to spend the rest of the night with him and when he woke up the next day he was half convinced he was madly in love.

* * *

She made him wait for three long days before according him her favors once more. She even seemed to be avoiding him... Then, on the morning they were supposed to go ashore in Cuba, he found a little note on his night table. She was telling him to pack his personal effects and a few clothes and to come and join her on the dock once he was ashore. Bernard wondered what she had in store for him... The possibilities that came instantly to mind were enough to produce an immediate bulge in his light cotton pants. He remembered all too well the unbelievable night he had spent with her.

She was waiting for him wearing a simple white dress and carrying a big canvas bag over her shoulder. Giving him a chaste little kiss on the cheek, she took him by the hand and guided him onboard the superb sailboat that was docked right beside the "Sea Queen". She explained that all three of them, Bernard, Valérie, and her friend Liana, the sailboat's owner, would be going to Key West. She would make sure that whatever belongings he still had onboard the cruise ship were sent anywhere he wished after that. “Eez that OK wiss you?” she asked him, as if he had a choice... How little she knew him.

The trio left Cuba even before the other passengers onboard the “Sea Queen” had even set foot on shore. They were sailing warm turquoise seas in this gorgeous craft, which was no cheap wooden shell either. Oh no! It was completely equipped with everything needed for a long voyage and could comfortably accommodate six people. Bernard quickly discovered that Valérie was in fact an accomplished sailor and her friend Liana was a highly competent (and appetizing!) captain. But he only had eyes for Valérie, his French girlfriend who was giving him every reason to believe, by her sly little winks and moist little kisses, that this was going to be one very pleasant trip indeed.

Liana was the opposite of Valérie. Of Cuban origin, she had jet black hair that cascaded down to her waist and her eyes were just as black. She was small and curvy and her bikini could barely contain her full, ripe breasts. Her hips, which swayed so charmingly when she walked, were nice and round (even a little on the wide side) and her shapely legs were solid but still graceful. She had smooth, fine-grained skin which was the color of wet sand and gave off a scent that was heavily fragrant like some rich, exotic fruit. Liana was paradise to look at but Bernard did not dare linger on her charms too much because he didn't want to displease his darling Valérie in any way. It was her who brought up the subject.

– Do you find her... beeyoutiful?

– Not as much as you...

– I find her very beeyoutiful... It is OK if you do too.

– Yes she is beautiful, in a very different way...

Having lost all sight of land now, they were alone in the world, lost in a universe of turquoise water, sea and sun. Bernard was swimming in happiness and hoped with all his heart that the good fairy would not choose this moment to transform him back into the pathetic creature he used to be. But he wisely decided not to linger on such somber thoughts and concentrate instead on the here and now: he was sailing blissfully away with the kind of girl he had always dreamed of, and another one who was looking more mouth-watering all the time... Why waste precious moments on worry when such a dream girl was sauntering nearly nude in front of him, offering iced beer, hot kisses and such silent but explicit promises?

The captain dropped anchor around noon and all three of them decided to take the plunge into this translucent wonder that surrounded them. Laughing mischievously like boisterous children, they removed all their clothing and dived into the deliciously warm water. They watched lovely colored creatures gliding by them for a while, and then Valérie swam up to him and said, somewhat shyly:

– Don't... be mad wiss me. It's just that I haven't seen Liana for such a long time...

This much said, she swam up to Liana and both of them started wrestling around, splashing and pinching each other, laughing hysterically all the while. After a while, they locked their arms around each other and began kissing... Passionately. Valérie's lips seemed to be drinking Liana's as they became more and more interlaced and their caressing became increasingly specific...

At this precise moment, Bernard, who was harder than

iron now, believed he had died and gone to heaven. Through the blessedly clear waters, he could see his cock reacting to this unexpected but highly desirable turn of events. He didn't dare approach them for fear of interrupting their escapade and breaking the magic spell. The sirens swam over to the sailboat so they could get some footing on the ladder all while keeping their bodies submerged. Valérie had a decided penchant for water!

Liana was now holding herself against the ladder and Valérie, who was gripping the rope, carefully rubbed her small firm breasts against Liana's bigger ones, while their hips gyrated together in a savage waltz that drove Bernard crazy. Their kisses were insistent, their teeth leaving little imprints on the bronzed skin they bit. Watching two incredible pairs of breasts pressed together that way, with nipples so stiff and erect, had a devastating effect on Bernard. He had to find a place to sit down or grab onto... otherwise he was going to drown on the spot. He was practically forgetting to breathe. The two women understood his distress as soon as they saw him approaching. Valérie flashed him an affectionate smile and gave Liana a sign to get back on board. The latter turned around, pausing for just a second so that Valérie could stroke her breasts some more before she finally resumed climbing.

She hadn't gone up three steps when Valérie grabbed hold of her and pulled her downwards again. Liana lifted one leg up so she could offer herself to her girlfriend, lowering her ample buttocks to make Valérie's task easier. Valérie buried her face between the other woman's tender, tawny thighs and licked her avidly with a greedy little tongue. It was too much! Bernard glued himself against Valérie's back with the firm intention of ramming his rock hard cock right inside of her. Someone had to teach her the consequences of parading such behavior in front of him... But she was one step ahead of him. She scrambled up the ladder after Liana, and he was left panting, treading water, and erect to the point of exploding. But the spectacular view he had of those two incomparable female behinds made him come to his senses and hurry after them.

Liana had thrown herself on top of a very willing Valérie and she now lay over the length of her body. They hugged furiously, rolling around one on top of the other, spreading each other's thighs apart with their legs, mashing their crotches together... Liana's huge breasts were squashing Valérie's tinier ones. Liana raised her chest and freed her partner's delicious little tits so she could begin gently licking and sucking them. Pulling herself up a little more, she spread Valérie's thighs apart and her hot tongue descended to teasingly lick her girlfriend. After a few minutes, she lay down on Valérie once more so that their legs, tongues and wet hair intermingled. "What a fabulous contrast of colors and textures!", thought Bernard in ecstasy.

Valérie chose that blessed moment to give him a sign to come closer, without, however, giving him permission to touch or stroke her. Spreading Valérie's pink lips apart with her dark fingers, Liana exposed her friend's shaved pussy to the hot rays of the sun, giving Bernard a stunning view of Valérie's swollen and palpitating clitoris. Liana began to eat her out in earnest now, considerately turning her head a little to one side so that Bernard could admire the show. After letting her tongue do the work for awhile, Liana pushed her agile fingers deep into Valérie's pussy, causing the latter to quiver ever so gently as she whispered both Bernard and Liana's names. She came almost immediately.

Bernard eyes were riveted on her dripping, helplessly contracting pussy and he desperately wanted a taste... which both women simultaneously refused.

His frustration was increasing at the same rate as his excitement, but his troubles weren't over yet... Valérie got up on her knees and pulled Liana towards her. They kissed with insatiable ardor and rubbed their breasts together again. Valérie's slender fingers began exploring the moist, sticky folds between Liana's legs. The Cuban then went to lie down on some piled up mattresses in the corner, Valérie following her like a good little kitty before kneeling down to taste the dark wetness between her lover's legs.

Nothing was going to stop Bernard now. There was no turning back. He was staring at Valérie's beautiful spread apart cheeks right in front of him and he didn't have to tell his cock twice to go join them. With one quick finger, he was able to assess that she was still very well lubricated and quite ready for the assault he was planning. Like a bull going for the matador, he went in for the attack, shoving himself inside of her with all his brute strength. He heard the urgent moan rising from the lips that were firmly planted on Liana's pussy. The view was spectacular from where he was. He watched himself thrusting into the blonde who was licking the brunette... He rammed Valérie hard with a volley of brutal thrusts before deciding to make the pleasure last as long as possible. He slowed down to savor the spectacle.

Valérie made them move to one side so that he could get a good look at Liana's gaping pussy. She was gleaming wet. Valérie fondled, pinched and affectionately nibbled her girlfriend's tawny breasts before returning to her task further down. The sight of her tanned fingers probing the other woman's dark, slick opening made Bernard shudder furiously as he pumped away. He couldn't speed up or touch himself or he would have exploded. Two pairs of knowledgeable hands were now running all over the Cuban's body. Valérie's hands were covering her breasts and hair, and Liana was fingering her own stomach and thighs. Bernard pulled out for a moment so he could get a clear eyeful of their glistening pussies. He wanted to taste both women now and savor the difference.

He invaded Valérie with an eager tongue that he flicked around inside of her. She sighed deeply and slid her hand between Liana's hot, humid thighs. Liana in turn penetrated Valérie with her long brown fingers. Knowing that his lover was now in good hands, Bernard slid his face between Liana's thighs. She had a sweeter, more mellow taste than Valérie, like some mysterious exotic spice. Valérie then decided to stretch her insatiable lover out on his back. Straddling him backwards, she lay down over his torso and took his cock in her mouth. Liana got up and knelt down over his face, suddenly flooding him with her orgasm as she shoved a distracted finger inside of Valérie. After a brief instant in which Bernard thought he might die of pleasure, Valérie freed him and stood up, making Liana lie down in front of her so she could return to tasting that sweetness between her lover's legs. As she fell to her knees and went down on Liana, Valérie offered her ass to a stupefied Bernard once more. He answered her call immediately and slid himself hard inside of her while Liana's fruity taste still swam in his mouth. He tried to hold himself back some more but in vain... His stomach muscles were refusing to cooperate any more; they began contracting with a vengeance, demanding the release of the most powerful orgasm of his life. But he was still determined to make the climax last as long as he possibly could...

In the middle of all this, Bernard suddenly realized that this escapade was probably just the first in a series of wonderful adventures that he would be experiencing over the course of the next few days. This vision took away his breath and his will. His brain went on strike, he was nothing but a helpless slave to his cock and balls now. He knew he was losing the battle, that he was going to finally let it all blow when...

SPLASH!!!

He found himself in the water... in the swimming pool. The first sensation he was aware of was his all too painful erection. He swallowed a ton of water and the chlorine stung his throat and went up his nose, making him gag and choke. Shaking his scanty haired head as he came to the surface, he realized with horror that a terrible sunburn covered the entire front of his pudgy body. His too-tight bathing suit was murdering his flabby waist and roasted thighs.

It was only at this moment that he came back to sad reality. The gang of idiots he called his friends were circling him in the water and laughing like maniacs. It was that big goof, Gerry, who finally said something:

– What the hell were you dreaming about, you big jerk? You must have had the hard-on of your life! There was actually a bump in your Speedo!

One Woman's Happiness...

Alex had been recounting her latest heartaches to Peter, a good friend and occasional lover. After listening to her tale of woe, and offering his solid shoulder for her to cry on or hit, Peter finally said:

– Don't worry my poor Alex, wisdom will come to grace you yet... You did nothing wrong except maybe walk into a situation with your eyes shut tight again..

The situation he was referring to was in fact one of the most maddening ones Alex had ever gotten herself into. During the course of her rather unstable love life, some episodes had been reasonably happy, some had been totally frustrating or just plain sad, and others had been nothing short of sensational. But this latest one took the cake!

Peter and Alex had been good friends since they had begun their studies together. He was one of the first people to receive the news of her engagement. He was there to cheer her on when she got married and to console her, fifteen years later, when she got divorced. Peter also actively witnessed the massive "identity crisis" that hit her the day she turned forty. That was approximately the time when they became lovers, three years ago already... Oh, it was nothing "serious" of course. Just two good friends who got along fine in bed and knew how to offer and receive the pleasure of consolation when times were tough.

The marriage and ensuing divorce were classic scenarios: Alex and Jerome had dated during their high school and university years. They were married as soon as they got their degrees, had a quiet life in the suburbs and then WHAM! Husband falls in love with a colleague sixteen years his junior and blames his wife for not remaining the adolescent he fell in love with. That seemed to be ample justification for him to simply go out and find another adolescent to replace her with.

She had tried to reason with him. She had suggested marriage counseling and had even proposed that Jerome spend time with "The Other Woman" so that he could properly weigh out the pros and cons. But it was all in vain. He had already made his decision and wanted the divorce to be pronounced as quickly as possible because his new flame felt wrong about settling down with a married man... "Talk about playing dirty!", Alex had raged, "Why didn't she just leave the married man alone in the first place?" But she concluded that this concept was probably too elaborate for the woman's tiny brain...

So... The days preceding her divorce had been spent feeling extremely sorry for herself, brooding incessantly over the idea that she was getting old and was no longer attractive. In short, her self-esteem hit the zero mark. If it hadn't been for Natalie... She would be grateful to Natalie for the rest of her life. This cherished friend had gone to great lengths to help Alex out of her stagnation. Natalie's ultimate therapy had included several excursions downtown to empty the clothing stores, a trip to the hairdresser and beautician, and a tour of all the trendiest bars to show Alex what an effect she still had on men. All in all, the results were very encouraging... She didn't meet the "soul mate" or encounter mad passion – something she had never really known anyway – but men were flirting with her all evening long and she had adored every instant of it. That bastard Jerome could go to hell! One morning, Alex made a firm decision to be on the look-out for every potential affair that might come her way, and to allow herself to indulge in every interesting fantasy that might surface in her life... After all, she deserved all the pleasure she could get her hands on, didn't she?...

There seemed to be a catch, however. None of these males in heat really stirred up any luscious desires in her... "Trust fate!", Natalie kept telling her, "It's when you least expect it that something will happen!" Easy to say... Well, it took a few years, but that something did happen; however, it wasn't quite what Alex had expected...

It was when this year's school started up again – the first day in fact – that she noticed Sebastian. Suddenly, there he was standing right in front of her. He was huge with shoulder length blond curls, reminding her of a Greek god. And his eyes... a jaw-dropping, beautiful green, with tiny gold specks. He could have been a model, a movie star, or a football player. But he had one remarkable quirk, all too rare, she was sure, in one so good-looking: he was adorably shy, and would blush crimson whenever talked to. She wasn't usually partial to men who were too perfect looking, but one glance at Sebastian took her breath away and produced instant stomach butterflies. He had actually managed to break her rock solid concentration! Amazing! She would have given anything at that moment to have been able to start stroking those incredible blond curls. To this day, she still remembers his classic reaction to her stare: completely unable to meet her eyes, he had given her a shy sideways smile and said nothing, as if the cat had swallowed his tongue, which would have been a shame...

At first, the promise of a liaison with Sebastian seemed like some sort of godsend. It was every female's dream come true: mutual love at first sight, or whatever came closest to it, and passion that needed only to be sparked to start smoldering into something impossible to resist. There you go! Alex knew in her heart that she had been just waiting for something like this to happen, but she also knew something else... She, who had shamelessly condemned her husband for acting like a latent adolescent, was now about to enter the same territory... And she had made such fun of Jerome! Sebastian was not a new teacher or even a student teacher. Oh no!, that would have been much too simple. He was a student and barely twenty years old! "Alex, my ancient Alex, you will wipe these lustful thoughts from your mind this instant!", she told herself sternly. And she did manage, for a time, to convince herself that she had actually regained control. At least for a little while...

During the next two weeks, she would find herself trying to cross paths with Sebastian in the hallway, or guiltily looking for him on the campus grounds. She was also tormented by renegade thoughts (e.g. him, naked, in her bed, coming at the top of his lungs...).

When he was in class, Alex would lose her concentration and forget where she was in the lecture she was giving to the pack of ignoramuses she suddenly didn't give a damn about. She knew this was an outright lack of professionalism, but these days, her desire was seriously undermining her self-discipline. As the young man's intense gaze slid all over her, she felt more and more convinced that the attraction was mutual. She would have given anything to feel his hands on her body, this body that was now causing her a lot of ambivalent feelings...

But it was unthinkable! Alex was a dedicated teacher. Her career was also her vocation, something she truly believed in.

One afternoon, Peter caught up with her in the cafeteria.

– How's it going? You don't look a hundred percent these days...

– Oh, it's OK. I'm just a little tired, that's all.

– Too much work?

– Oh no! I'm a little preoccupied and I haven't been sleeping or eating that well... nothing serious.

– You're not sick, are you?

Peter looked worried.

– No, no... I'm just a little distracted, that's all.

He was quiet for a moment and then he addressed her with a sly little smile:

– Hum... There wouldn't by any chance be a man behind all this, would there?

– Why would you say that?

Her answer had a touch of irritation she hadn't meant to convey, but she felt herself blushing nonetheless. She suddenly blurted:

– Just because I'm a little preoccupied doesn't mean there has to be a man involved! What's gotten into you? You're all so egocentric! If a women gets distracted, there has to be a man involved, right!?

– Hey, hey, relax! No problem... I'll leave you alone now! When you've calmed down, we'll talk again. See you later, Alex!

– Peter, wait!

But he had already gone towards a group of teachers that Alex didn't feel like joining right now. She would have to apologize to him later.

It was only in the middle of the afternoon that she found him in his office. After sheepishly entering the room, she softly said to him:

– I'm sorry. I'm a bundle of nerves...

– What's up? Do you want to go have a coffee? I've got an hour to kill before the next class.

– OK, let's go!

Initially, she had no intention of sharing her sordid preoccupations with him; at any rate, she was burning with shame about it. Was she in the process of stumbling into the footsteps of some of her male colleagues who embarked on risky affairs? The same colleagues she had always referred to as "lecherous old pigs"? But, as always, she was underestimating Peter's instincts about her. He knew damn well that the only reason she had flown off the handle that day was because he had hit the nail right on the head and he was bristling with curiosity now. Alex took the plunge and told him the entire story. There was a heavy silence at the end of it and she didn't even dare look at Peter for fear of instant judgment and condemnation. After what seemed like an eternity, he lifted her chin and asked her with a mysterious smile:

– And what are you going to do about this?

– Nothing! Nothing at all! I'm twice his age... It's unthinkable! Can you imagine what they'd say about me?

– Oh, they would probably say that you really know how to have a good time and you couldn't give a damn what other people think! If you really want my opinion, I think that attitude is a lot more in keeping with the Alex I know. And if it bothers you to that extent, all you have to do is be discreet.

– You're nuts! I'm old enough to be his mother! And

what would it really accomplish in the end? He'd eventually meet someone else and just dump me. All that anguish for nothing...

– And what makes you think, once you conquer him with your fine mind and your charm, that he might not want a serious relationship?

– You're dreaming my friend! But I know the way this stuff works... I'm going to stay obsessed with him until I can find some way of living it out...

– Go on then! What have you got to lose?

– My reputation, maybe?

– Which one? The reputation for spending all your nights alone lusting in vain after some young body?

Alex had a terrible urge to hit him at this moment. Why didn't she just go for it and plow him one? Probably because of that stupid little smile on his endearing little mug. And maybe he wasn't so off base after all? What did she really have to lose?

The next morning, she didn't avert her gaze from Sebastian's, and she gave him the most engaging smiles. She would apply this tactic for awhile to see whether or not there was a favorable response from him. It was one thing to imagine a relationship with a mere boy, quite another thing to make him take the bait...

This game continued for about two more weeks, but there were some promising turns. He now stopped to talk to her after every class. Their discussions usually revolved around the course content, but he did release a few facts about his personal life as well. She now knew certain details about him like: Al Pacino was his idol and swimming was his passion (hence the magnificent body...) but he had been forced to stop training a year ago because of a serious leg injury.

All in all, things were definitely moving forward, at a snail's pace to be sure, but moving forward nonetheless. The whole situation was, however, increasing her distraction and her dreams were becoming decidedly more perverse. She dreamt that he was waiting for her every day at her house, stretched lasciviously out on her bed, wearing only loose silk shorts. And of course it went further than that... The caressing began, each move more daring than the next until he was soon bending her in positions worthy of an acrobat. In each one of these dreams, Sebastian would catapult her into dizzying heights of pleasure, spinning her around on his disproportionate member, giving her orgasm after orgasm. She would wake up dripping with sweat. The most troubling thing was that the dreams didn't only invade her mind during the night anymore. In the middle of a course, Alex would find herself taking advantage of rare moments of student concentration to start dreaming up new athletic positions she could twist her young lover's body into. At night when she was at home, she would masturbate slowly, creating detailed fantasies of what they would do together. He would watch her stroking herself as he stood a little timidly to one side, then his state of arousal would soon match hers and he would finally come and join her...

One afternoon, after a quick sandwich with Peter, she chose to wander outside to grade her test papers so she could enjoy the beautiful fall day (and be available to her students just in case...). She sat down on a bench in the sun but soon found herself unable to concentrate for even one sentence. Closing her eyes, she just let her mind drift. The cool breeze that ruffled her hair suddenly became a gentle wind blowing across a New-England beach where she and Sebastian were walking together hand in hand. After a few greedy kisses, he led her towards one of the huge Victorian mansions that were scattered on the shoreline. It was a magnificent house, all pink and blue... They made love in a sky-lit bedroom on a gigantic brass bed with embroidered sheets, to the sound of huge raindrops splashing on the roof overhead... He ran his hands all over her, lifting her hips as if she was light as a feather and then gently entering her, fixing his intense green eyes on hers before beginning to thrust. He started out gently but was soon shoving harder and harder until they were moving at such an infernal rate that the massive bed began bumping towards the middle of the room...

– Hello!

Alex jumped as if someone had pricked her with something. Adrenaline surged through her body, causing her heart to pound dangerously for a few seconds. Standing right in front of her was the object of her fantasies, looking more incredible than ever.

– Hel-hello!

– May I sit down?

– Yes, of course... No classes now?

– No, not until tomorrow afternoon.

– It's so nice out, isn't it...

Then, as if inspiration had suddenly struck him, he asked her:

– Do you bicycle?

– Sometimes. Why?

– I know you have one more class to give. Uh, I mean...

The adorable blushing started up but he stumbled on:

– If you'd like, a little later on we could get together and go for a ride along the river. Well, it was just an idea... I'm going to go for a ride anyway, but if you'd like to join me, I mean... it would be more fun...

Alex was pleased to note that he had studied her schedule...

– What a great idea! But I'm not super fit. If you promise not to go too fast...

– I'm not planning to race you!

It was just as simple as that... The opportunity she had been lusting after for weeks and had started to believe would never arise had just transpired in an almost mundane way. A simple invitation, a simple acceptance, that was it! They met at four o'clock on the bridge that led to the deserted little island in the middle of the river. The bicycle path that snaked around the island was about twenty kilometers long. It was a charming, and almost deserted setting now that it was late afternoon. The island had lots of hills and trees and some of the leaves were already turning to warm autumn colors. They were pedaling side by side, slowly enough for amiable chatting, when they suddenly came upon a park midway through the island. It was a very pretty and very inviting location right by the river's edge. Sebastian suddenly seemed a bit nervous when they dismounted from their bicycles. He obviously had something to say, and it was making him uneasy.

– Alex, I have something I want to ask you. I don't really know how to begin, and I hope you won't take it the wrong way... But, well, is this something you have a habit of doing normally, you know, doing things like bicycle riding with one of your students?

He was staring at her from the corner of one eye and was visibly uncomfortable now.

– Well actually, Sebastian, this is the first time. Why do you ask?

Alex was every bit as nervous as he was, if not more so,

but she was fighting hard not to let it show.

– Because Alex, well!... I have a little problem. I don't know anything about you or your private life, but...

He wrung his hands and stared at the river.

– Since classes began, I've been asking myself some very strange questions. It's probably my imagination, but it seems to me... at least I hope that... Uh!...

He took a quick deep breath before continuing:

– Well, it's just that... I'd like to get to know you better... I think you're wonderful, brilliant, and since the first day I saw you I've been thinking about you... Uh! You must think I'm an idiot. You probably consider me a teenager, just another student among so many other students... I... uh...

– Sebastian, you're not just another student for me... I've got to admit that I've been thinking about you too ever since classes began. And probably not in the way you'd imagine either...

– That's pretty much what I thought... "Not the way I imagined...". OK, you don't have to say any more. I'm sorry for all this juvenile awkwardness. How could I have been crazy enough to imagine that someone like you might be interested in me...

– You've got it all wrong! I am interested! And I thought I was the crazy one for dreaming that a beautiful, bright young guy like you would be interested in someone twice his age. Surely, there can't be a shortage of university girls who would give anything to be with you?

With no warning at all, Sebastian sealed his mouth over hers and silenced her on the spot. Even at that moment she still found herself wanting to balk at a situation that continued to trouble her. But his kiss was insistent, and the stunning rush of pleasure it brought her broke down all remaining resistance. She released herself into the bliss of tasting him and soon became just as demanding as him. She felt like a teenager experiencing her first kiss in secret, and she was reacting with an ardor she had never felt before... He squeezed her in his powerful arms, kneading her back and shoulders with rough caresses. Months of abstinence now induced violent surges of desire in Alex and she found herself gasping for breath in the merciless grip of uncontainable passion. She wanted to bite that mouth, wrap those golden curls around her fingers, consume this strong young body that she had been dreaming of for so long now. Her breasts began to swell, her thighs began to burn and her lower belly was contracting with desire. She had almost forgotten the worries she had concerning this young man whose clothes she wanted to rip off, whose body she wanted to straddle and ride like a demon...

She opened her eyes just a fraction and saw an older couple heading towards a bench not far from where she and Sebastian were now lying on the ground groping away. She pulled herself away from him like a schoolgirl caught in the wrong and got up to go lean against the balustrade at the water's edge where she stared tensely at the river flowing by. Sebastian came and joined her but didn't dare stand too close to her. When he finally spoke, he sounded very uneasy.

– I'm sorry... It was stronger than me.

She turned to look at him in surprise.

– Sorry? I'm not... Listen Sebastian, I didn't exactly put up a fight did I...? I've been wanting to do that for over a month now. But I'm confused. I can't get my brain around it. What is it that you want from me? What do you expect? A one night stand? I can only visualize something like that... And I'm not exactly sure what it is that I want from this. I think I want the whole deal... but I'm frightened... I'm afraid you'll just end up meeting some pretty young student your own age and then send me off to pasture. I'm afraid of looking ridiculous... I'm afraid, but I want to, so much...

– You're asking yourself far too many questions. Right now, we both want to be together. And with girls my own age, I pretty much lose interest after about a week. I need something more. I need a woman, a real woman who's going to be more than just a bed partner. A woman I can really talk to about anything, who can talk to me too. And not just about actors and rock stars or fashion... I want you. We have no way of knowing what will happen two months, two years or even twenty years down the line. No one knows that. What have we really got to lose? Is it so much more than any other couple starting out?

"What have we really got to lose?" It seemed she had heard this one about a hundred times in the last month, but her last remaining scruples melted right then and there. Her eyes dove into the young man's as she kissed him firmly on his full, soft lips. Without a word, the couple returned to their bicycles and headed back for the city. Sebastian rode up beside her and took her hand.

– Will you follow me?

– I'm following.

He lived in a loft in the old part of the city. The immense space was bathed in the light of the setting sun that poured abundantly through the big windows. Closing the door behind them, he took her in his arms and they quickly resumed where they had left off in the park. He picked her up by her hips with one arm while his other hand began busily undoing the buttons of her blouse. Alex felt so tiny compared to him; he was lifting her up with no strain at all. All the dreams and fantasies she had been harboring for so long came flooding back to her... She couldn't let go of his big, comforting shoulders; she wanted to stay attached to him forever. Running her small hands over his tightly muscled back, she finally twisted her fingers through his silken curls. He carried her over to a large mattress tossed on the floor and very gently placed her down on it, kneeling beside her as he did.

Those brilliant green eyes were staring at her intensely as he brought his face close to hers...

– Are you OK? Have you changed your mind?

– If you stop now, you fail your course...

As Sebastian pulled her face towards him, forcing her to look him in the eye, Alex read a mixture of expressions on his face: curiosity, slyness, desire and even a hint of pain... A violent shiver ran through her. After so many months with no body contact, her belly now felt like it was being ripped apart by desire! Her remaining fears finally lost their grip on her and she became totally defiant instead. She would accord herself this pleasure, however brief it would be, consequences be damned! She begged him to undress in front of her. He blushed furiously, but he did get up, slowly pulling off his sweater so she could admire his supple, well-toned torso and superb stomach muscles. He was nicely tanned, just the right depth; it was the golden hue of someone who spends a lot of time outdoors. He sat down on the bed for an instant and Alex fell against his amazing, V-shaped back, wrapping herself around him as she slid herself down to his slender waist. My god, he was beautiful! She had never seen a body like his, except maybe in an art gallery... He slid off his pants to reveal his perfect, adorably untanned behind. His erection was impressive as well... It didn't have the excessive proportions to be found in Alex's heated fantasies, but it was more than respectable. Laying back down on the bed, he asked her to undress for him. She took his arms and told him gently:

– I'm not twenty anymore... Come here.

He didn't insist. Instead, he pulled away her blouse and moved down to undo her pants, slowly sliding them down her thighs as he proceeded to kiss every new inch of exposed skin. When she was finally nude, he looked her over from head to foot.

– You're really beautiful, you know! More beautiful than I even imagined...

He lay on top of her, covering the frailer Alex with his massive body as he hugged her hard. She was impatient though... She wanted to feel him inside of her, to be liberated at last from her burden of solitude. But he chose to make her wait. Sliding his hands under her, he lifted her up, leaving only her shoulders to rest on the bed. Alex's legs were spread so the young man could kiss her thighs, sliding his tongue up her leg until it brushed against her famished pussy. He then placed her back down over his folded legs and grabbed her waist. His large hands began massaging her, traveling up her body until they reached her shoulders, pulling them up so he could kiss her face, eyes and neck... She begged him to make love to her...

Instead, he gently laid her legs back down on the bed and got up. Alex watched as he headed over to a dresser and pulled a flask out of a drawer. Bringing it back with him, he knelt between the legs she had parted in offering and told her to close her eyes. The sun's heat warmed her shivering skin, and then she felt something rich and oily being poured between her breasts and down her belly. Sebastian dabbed a few fingers in this fragrant oil and gently rubbed it over her nipples and breasts, gradually moving to her shoulders, arms, armpits, and then down to her belly... He poured a little more oil over the sides of her waist, causing her little shivers of pleasure, and then he moved further down still until he reached her now gaping lips. She was startled by the sensation of his fingers tracing the contours of her vulva. She felt the oil mixing with her own sweet dew and smelt the heat charged odor that ensued. Laying down on top of her again, he rubbed his skin against hers to anoint himself, sliding himself all over Alex's body as she took the opportunity to slather some oil herself onto his gorgeous back. Sebastian picked up the bottle again and pulled his teacher's pelvis a little closer towards him. His hands descended her abdomen and slowly, ever so slowly, he inserted a finger inside her while his tongue savored the creamy mixture that now bathed her inner thighs. When Sebastian's lips finally rested on her pussy, it felt like an electric shock. Determined to drive her insane with desire, it seemed, he tickled her with his tongue, his hands still flowing over her lustrously oiled body. He became completely focused, tasting every part of her with his hot wet mouth as if her flesh was the tenderest, tastiest fruit. When he finally sensed the time was right, he pulled her up from the bed and made her lean against the wall. Without any apparent effort, he lifted her up and delicately placed her pussy over the tip of his tautly erect penis, sliding her down on top of him as he impaled her very slowly, millimeter by millimeter.

Alex couldn't get enough of him... She went crazy for his mouth, his taste, his skin, his amazing shoulders, the untiring arms that held her up and guided her inside him. After a rapturous slide, she felt the full length of him crammed inside of her. Staying very still, he was content to just watch her for a moment. Then he smiled and kissed her as he began to lift her up and down over his cock in a tantalizing rhythm. Her legs were wrapped around his waist now, and as she gripped his body, she felt her oiled and stiffly erect nipples being crushed against his chest. Alex's body floated against his as if it had lost all substance and was now submerged in a soft warm cloud. They were moaning in unison as Sebastian sped up his rhythm, and they came together in a shuddering, mind-blowing climax.

Every night after this, for close to three weeks, they would meet at his place or hers, and each encounter seemed more extraordinary than the last. They would spend entire nights making exquisite love in every conceivable position, using every imaginable technique...

* * *

Alex began to suspect that something wasn't right when he began arriving late for their rendez-vous. His excuses were always plausible, but his eyes betrayed him... Then he began spacing out their meeting times. She became utterly convinced that what she had dreaded since the beginning was now in the process of happening: he would drop her soon for a younger, sexier, much more fresh-faced girl. One evening, she finally decided to confront him. They had been making love for quite a while but she knew all too well that his thoughts were elsewhere. Feeling like her heart might give out, she asked him point blank if he had met someone his own age that he wanted to be with. There was irritation in his answer:

– No! Not at all! What do you think I'd want with some young ditz? Cut it out. I've already told you that stuff does nothing for me.

Had she said or done something wrong? Alex tried to be rational. Maybe he just needed more space. But one evening, when they were supposed to go to the movies together and he didn't show up, she finally lost it. She was convinced she knew exactly what was wrong. He didn't dare tell her, she supposed, knowing that she had already gone through the same ordeal with the only other important man in her life. "Oh well! Too bad!", she told herself with false conviction. She would go to the movies without him, and once he decided to confess the truth about his new liaison, at least this time she would be prepared. As she walked towards the theater with a confident stride, she felt relief in knowing that it would be her this time, and not someone else saying: "I told you so!"

The night was clear and cool and it took Alex no time to cover the short distance between her house and the theater. There were no crowds and she quickly entered the cinema and found a seat. Leaving her sweater there, she then went to get a drink. That's when she saw him. His back was turned from her, and there he was with his newest conquest. She wasn't much taller than Alex... Even though Alex couldn't see her face, she was already sure that this woman couldn't be more than eighteen or nineteen. She felt gut sickening devastation at seeing her worst fears materialize, but her shock was also tinged with mute incomprehension. She felt that annoying cliché surface unbidden inside of her, that palliative phrase that all women refer to at least once in their lives in an attempt to surmount their pain: "What has she got that I don't have?" And she honestly couldn't find any answers to that question. He could have chosen among innumerable tall, thin, gorgeous students. But this woman was definitely on the short side, and she certainly wasn't on the thin side... She was wearing jeans that did absolutely nothing for her rear end and when Sebastian pulled her up to kiss her and nibble her neck, Alex could see that this tiny person also had to ridiculously perch on tiptoe to reach his face. But this wasn't the worst part...

When the couple turned around to go back into the theater, the shock Alex received was like a punch in the stomach and then a slap across the face...

The time she had spent with him had been incredible. She had always known from the start that it would be a transitory affair. Even the searing jealousy she felt now had been anticipated for awhile. It had only been a matter of time... But what knocked the wind out of her and destroyed her on the spot was the fact that she actually knew the woman he was with right now... And this creature hanging off his arm in such a pathetic fashion was anything but a pretty young thing... Alex and she weren't friends. Far from it... Not only was she no model or beauty queen, she was probably the very last person Alex expected to see with him. This was a woman who boasted about needing no one... A woman who endlessly ranted to all who would listen that casual affairs were poison...

And here she was, exposing her hypocrisy for all to see! She had usurped Sebastian, this young man who had taught Alex so much, right out from under her. She was no more pretty or attractive than the last time Alex had seen her. That had been at about the same time last year when Alex, Peter and a few others had been gathered together by a mutual friend to celebrate this woman's birthday... her forty ninth.